The Girl with the Black Lipstick

The Girl with the Black Lipstick

Mary Biddinger

A Novella-in-Flash

www.blacklawrence.com

Executive Editor: Diane Goettel
Cover & Book Design: Amy Freels
Cover Art: "Chestnut Street, Chicago 2013, 2024" by Satoki Nagata

ISBN: 978-1-62557-161-8

Published 2025 by Black Lawrence Press.
Printed in the United States.

For all the roommates.

Contents

I don't miss the city. I miss the place it was in the nineties, when everyone else also was twenty-two and broke.

—Sarah Manguso, *300 Arguments*

Quake of Recognition

I can't help but wonder if my graduate school roommate is somewhere in the galaxy watching *Russian Doll*, thinking its episodic nature resembles some of our most memorable vignettes. That morning when we met with the nun who was supposed to take us back to the shudders of the womb—what if we returned decades later in the same clothes and asked the same questions?

I'm shocked we never cataloged our worries. It was 1999 and everything was different. One time a fledgling blue jay flopped into the diner and I caught it in my skirt, then had to walk my hot pink panties to the street. One night I tried the three wise men shot and picked a fight with a pleasure boat operator regarding the color of the human heart.

I wonder if my roommate is now a spectral twin of my current self, taking too much joy in deadheading a slob geranium, encoding literary interview responses with cryptic references to our most noteworthy escapades. In the old days we both felt fragile, but we were actually at our best, an epiphany that makes me want to slit the throat of every ravioli in the pot.

The stupidest things make me sick now, like toothpaste and jumping. In the absence of the internet, my roommate and I used to huddle at Borders in sweatshirts and read all the books about nausea and inflammation. We would have interpreted the term "clickbait" as the best way to land some illegal smelt in the canal. Watched ridiculous talk shows with bubblegum pink press-on nails and a shared box of Sno-Caps.

It relieves me to know that someone else lives in our apartment now.

Lady of the Canal

We're on Lakeshore Drive, in one of those SUV taxis with flames painted on the sides. Next stop: every museum, followed by the architectural boat tour only booked by tourists with zero knowledge of architecture. Under the blue awning, riverside, I crack a joke about "Wacker Drive." My outfit a cross between accidental soft butch and academic drifter. Overalls pocket stuffed with food co-op receipts. Boots a little too industrial.

My roommate is dressed as a French nanny who smokes Djarums and speaks shockingly proficient English. We leer at couples redeeming coupons torn from the *Entertainment Book*. It's probably a two-drink minimum. Back then nobody looks at their cell phone unless placing a call. I worry that I forgot to wear deodorant, then brace myself against a bench, laughing. My roommate pesters the captain with targeted questions about the SS *Eastland* disaster. He's disquieted, but into it. A waterlogged pair of sweatpants licks the gangway.

We're code switching into French, then heading to the bathroom, which is more like an ice fishing shanty. I'm peeling off my corset while guarding the door. My roommate and I swap wigs, and I become a silver blonde who owns a speedboat named *Lady of the Canal*. In the distance: hairy thigh of the Swissôtel, where someone's husband drops his watch into an ashtray, unbuckles his belt while thinking of me. We've exceeded the two-drink minimum, and I order a cider, having no knowledge of which kind fits my persona except *hard*.

Story about the Sea

When I couldn't sleep, my roommate told me a story about the sea. A man named Perry stood on a dock sipping well water from a metal cup. The sea had dreams about tasting Perry's legs but never shared this desire with anyone (except my roommate). At the inciting incident of the story, with zero foreshadowing, Perry was tossed like a duffle of garbage from a barge.

When the sea stole each of Perry's garments separately—the fisherman's flannel, green wide-wale corduroy trousers, Saint Christopher medal, "wife-beater" undershirt that seemed anachronistic—I was either asleep or riveted enough to demand another chapter. My roommate pretended to close the book (the entire time turning imaginary pages) and slide it under my futon, where I stored hats that I was too embarrassed to wear in public.

When we put in our brunch reservation at Orange Blossom Café, it was *Perry, table for two*. Arriving early to a nightclub, we avoided suburban dickheads by talking about our friend Perry, his exercise regime involving handcrafted dry cell batteries and protein powder spun into cotton candy. My roommate promised a freshman comp class that one day Perry would show up as a substitute. They would know him as soon as they saw him.

When the sea finished threading Perry's bootlaces through the wreckage of the SS *Alpena*, it decided to style his hair in the fashion of Jim Morrison. On land, it was hard to tell if Perry's hair was gorgeous or simply dirty. At this juncture, my roommate broke the fourth wall with a critique of the cliché of sailors loving the sea like a woman. Perry was a notoriously poor lover, but the sea forgave him, and he flattened his face against every wave's trough.

One for the Record Books

They were pulling another body out of the canal. It didn't stop the fishermen nearby, or rollerblading couples holding hands, or seabirds dismantling a Doritos bag. "That body could have been somebody's roommate," I whispered into my roommate's armpit, which was about where I landed if no heels were involved.

Meanwhile the heat inched toward records. Forecasters in a constant state of near-orgasm over it, deploying the most ornate puns, thematically coordinated wardrobe choices. Somebody on the street asked my roommate if it was "hot enough."

We chose our apartment based on the lake breeze, but the landlord exaggerated, and so on the hottest days we slept heel to heel on vintage bathroom tile, wondering which vaudeville starlets of yesteryear might have drowned in our tub. Or perhaps that was just me wondering. My roommate had a complicated relationship with both history and ghosts.

My thoughts kept returning to the canal like a persistent trickle of wastewater. The early morning news featured a forecaster in a Santa costume brandishing a hair dryer. I startled to the sound of the kitchen on fire, but it was only my roommate making me toad in a hole, handwashing my favorite slip in a bucket of Tide.

Hot Tears

Summer school is like a bikini worn in place of underwear, so we both enrolled. It had something to do with loans, or preservation of health clinic privileges, or expedited graduation, or our resolution to combat ennui with extreme productivity. At first we decided on a poetry workshop, then changed our minds and took advanced memoir, which appealed to the one of us who was an extrovert much more than the introvert who blushed when a sliver of underwear was visible at the back of summer trousers.

Around this time the abnormally large butterflies were spotted in various parts of our city, including the rooftop deck that made me cry every time I climbed up there, west side steeples being too much even without three glasses of Rioja on an empty stomach. My roommate wasn't from Chicago, so it was just another deck with a view, but the butterflies evoked something primal, and we vowed to read *Love in the Time of Cholera* aloud to each other every evening before bed like mother and child.

I was wearing my mint green sundress to death, despite my roommate's advisement. When we distributed the first round of workshop essays mine had a strong effect on several classmates' gag reflexes, which signaled success. But it was my roommate's essay that caused our professor to blast a round of hot tears onto the seminar table, like how my Polly Potty doll of yesteryear leaked with enthusiasm. Jack, who always sat by the door, stood up and put on his leather jacket—my roommate's essay was that compelling.

The only other workshop triumph would be a case of contagious diarrhea experienced—I hoped—thanks to my second essay ("How to Blow Time"), but my roommate figured it was due to the undercooked dumplings Sondra brought as a sort of reverse ice breaker. On the way to class, we'd observed one of the enormous butterflies deceased in a drained memorial fountain. It made me want to get plastered in its honor.

Unknown Genesis

One day my roommate's aesthetic shifted, inexplicably, to bluegrass. A banjo arrived from an unknown origin. I had a peculiar rash from the lake, but blamed the music, which pervaded my sinuses. My roommate was wearing white denim bib overalls and attempting something weird with perm solution.

I was hate-writing a win-back story about a woman who goes back to her shitty ex-boyfriend because he never finished telling her a complicated joke about the inside of a jewelry box. Microsoft Works 3.0 could not keep up with the burning stream of my narrative. In the next room, my roommate melted a sardine tin into dance taps for a pair of wingtips of unknown genesis. The fumes were overwhelming, but I claimed it was the music making me dizzy, and then collapsed into a wall of bookshelves without knocking anything over.

At the emergency room, my roommate produced some kind of comfort blankie with a scarecrow print and ample fringe. Talked the charge nurse into accepting a bento box lunch in exchange for an orange priority sticker on my file. I figured it would be excellent research for my win-back story, in which the protagonist accidentally blows a Cheeto-thick line of coke and then forgets how to swallow, or something like that.

When commanded to remove my nameplate necklace (*Baby Girl*) my roommate worked the clasp with such panache that everyone thought we were a couple. The loser in my story would contemplate calling her shitty ex-boyfriend from the inpatient unit just to let the hospital phone number flash on caller ID. From the hospital window I could see a man burning several unopened packages of tube socks in a metal trash can. Or was he burning a banjo? I spent a lot of time really looking at my fingers.

The One Where We Pretend to Be Lincoln Park Trixies at Brunch

Lulu is certain she will never find permanent love. Permanent love, she claims, feels like the opposite of love ninety percent of the time.

Nobody responds, but my roommate rips open a pouch of Big League Chew. Thankfully we're on the front patio at Toastmakers and not in the packed dining room, since I have an aversion to bubble gum fragrance.

Violet claims that she's in love right now, but she is always in love, a true romantic who asks for a wedding dress for Christmas every year.

"The menu at Toastmakers has taken a shit," my roommate says. None of us knows how to interpret this remark. We're all buzzed thanks to appletinis on an empty stomach.

I'm unusually emotional because of my jelly shoes, which remind me of the pair I had in second grade. From the roof deck of Toastmakers we could probably glimpse my old elementary school twenty miles south, but we arrived too late to grab one of those prime tables.

My roommate asks our server about the temperature of the toasting tiles. Are they ceramic or cast iron? Was the yeast for the bread collected in a forest? Were the yeast collectors respectful?

They've probably never seen me wearing a ponytail prior to this day. Lulu held my shoulders while my roommate swept the hair up (didn't bother trying to brush through the ends) and wrangled elastic. The rest of the getup was easy to assemble.

We catch Violet batting eyelashes at a man watering a sidewalk catalpa.

Lulu seems natural in her yellow Chanel-adjacent thrifted shift. After my encounter with a haunted corset in undergrad, I have to be the first owner of all my clothes, the only exception a boyfriend's flannel or roommate's luxury cotton tank.

We keep waiting for someone to walk past Toastmakers, recognize us, snap a few photos, then run away laughing. Maybe we'll end up on the *Chicago Reader* talk of the town page.

But nobody walks by and says look at these trashy goths pretending to be Lincoln Park Trixies. After a while I stop shielding my tattoos with the issues of *Cosmo* we've lugged along.

I start to make a self-deprecating remark about my dissertation committee, then reconsider.

When the server finally realizes I haven't ordered my brunch yet, I ask for the pea sprout toast, which isn't toast at all.

A Very Decent Life

A cat can have a very decent life in an apartment, especially with roommates who compose regular fan letters to the wild salmon vendor. I was hogging the bathtub again, so my roommate ran downstairs to the lobby restaurant to use their outlets. We were heading to Venetian Night to see the illuminated boats and talk tourists out of being patriotic. Did they think it was a festival of mini blinds? Did they reckon the El was short for elephant? My roommate had been to Italy so many times that the anecdotes blurred into one psychedelic slideshow of tangling with strangers on the subway and shopping for antique shoes at dawn.

A cat can have a favorite roommate, and technically ours did not, but she only bathed with one of us. When I started grad school, I was really concerned about things like grout discoloration and sharpness of my pedagogy. Two years in, and I was letting students dig through my purse for entertainment while we spatter-painted some flocked wallpaper and called it multimodal discourse.

One day I was really down: somebody had called me "dizzy" as an insult, and I started sobbing right there in the seminar room. But then my roommate ordered an assortment of balloons delivered by "singing cow" to the main office, where I was second-guessing the firmness with which I'd filled out my final grades triplicate form.

I felt like an incomplete bubble pressed with a dull pencil as I made excuses into the phone to prevent my stupid boyfriend from meeting us at Venetian Night. Impromptu shellfish allergies, gnat warning, premonition of pickpockets who targeted former quarterbacks turned literary theorists. It was rough out there. My roommate finished buckling our cat's sequined peacoat, and we stomped out the door with our dignity.

The Opposite of Quaint

Today's roommates have it easy when it comes to holidays. Now it's perfectly acceptable to pass the holiest of evenings with shots of wheatgrass-flavored vodka, an inebriated crochet contest, storytelling by glow of flashlight entombed in red plastic wrap. In 1999, we were still required to begrudgingly board a train like minor characters in Russian novels, heading to the ancestral home for a thorough scourging. My steamer trunk contained garments I had left there since the last visit: pastel sweater sets, Keds, pajamas with bottoms.

As we loaded me into the cab, my roommate counted oblong pills into my change purse: two per day, plus one for emergency. My hair freshly trimmed and French braided, twin baguettes in my backpack, eyebrows sculpted and then penned: all the handiwork of my roommate, who might have been tearful as the taxi steered into traffic blasting Foghat. At the same time, I was envious of my roommate's stack of boarding passes, midnight phone calls in Québécois, metallic garments hanging in dry cleaner bags.

My ancestral home was liminal, and most of the walls were torn out for renovation, so guests lingered in load-bearing corridors while disassembling the micro-quiche. I dialed my apartment phone number just to listen to the answering machine, which my roommate updated to a robot-voice about *holiday* and *leave-taking*.

Someone who might have been an aunt asked my name and age. We had to descend to the first floor to access drinking water, doled out in stumpy carafes. The thermostat of my ancestral home hovered at

58 degrees year-round, but I suspected some of the wood beams were frozen, my bedding punitively rough like repurposed rice sacks. Five hours in and I was on pill number four, and had found all the affirmation cards my roommate tucked inside paired socks.

Nowadays when I'm reading a column about festive macaroni suppers for two, conjuring homemade snow in a pickle jar, or cauterizing sugar cookies into whimsical shapes, history feels the opposite of quaint. As I stepped into the pressure shower, towels of my family members slung over yet another temporary wall, I yearned to drown the new year before it hatched, but instead composed a letter to my roommate in my head, beginning with the lyrics to "Eight Days on the Road."

The One Where We Visit a Fortune Teller and Regret It

My roommate's aunt thought my name was Mariah and always sent us the most glorious holiday gift baskets. We never had to fight over the spoon-ready pears or portfolio of decadent brittles. Plenty to go around, even some to share with Josh across the hall, who kept an eye on our mailbox. My roommate peeled two luxury seedless mandarins at once, knowing the segments would never go to waste. I sunk my front teeth into a cookie known in my old neighborhood as a "kolachky" but labeled in a gold box as a "heavenly medallion."

Sometimes the gift baskets included a wild card item or two. I wondered if my roommate's aunt requested those things, or if they were extras tossed in by the gift basket assembler, like infinite vials of khaki bro cologne at the bottom of my box from Macy's. Along with our Halloween gourmet nut roll and scarecrow fingertip towels we found a mysterious gel in a bedazzled tube. We were not sure if it was a condiment or an ointment. My roommate slipped it into a kid's trick or treat bag when we ran out of fun-size Snickers.

Unpacking our combination Christmas and New Year's basket, my roommate discovered a set of Naughty Mrs. Claus thank you notes, a "kitty teaser" feather toy (presumably for our two beloved felines), and an unmarked business envelope nestled under paper hay. Inside, a gift certificate that smelled like nag champa. Two weeks later we were at a fortune teller's studio above Radio Shack. I prepared myself to be enlightened or murdered.

I'd seen TV fortune tellers recline on velour divans and choreograph the breeze, scores of candles swaying with every revelation. As sharp contrast, this fortune teller's waiting room was reminiscent of 24 Hr Cashland, our neighborhood desperation shop. Rigid plastic chairs, clipboards like the methadone clinic, small kids racing around annoyed customers. Fifteen minutes before our appointment time I began to feel itchy. My roommate showed zero signs of distress, so I tried not to scratch, but soon found myself consumed with twinges on my ankles and shoulders.

The gift certificate was for one session, couples welcome, which seemed normal until the receptionist pushed a red button and a man in pink scrubs led us back to the fortune teller's chamber. I wasn't sure if the door was actually locked—two booger-laden toddlers had cranked it after their mother vanished, leaving them with what appeared to be an older sister—or if the red button was to make clients feel safe with their secrets.

My roommate always went first when we visited haunted houses or academic advising drop-in hours, but I was already on my feet rubbing against a coat rack when we got buzzed back, so took the lead. The man in pink scrubs didn't look at either of us.

"Yep, it's our first time here. Christmas gift. Gift basket. Many pears," I said to him.

"My aunt is a tasteful shopper," my roommate offered, "single, eccentric, one of those people who will likely be discovered years after she dies on her couch."

At this moment my roommate's aunt stepped through a doorway of hanging beads, wearing heavy black crepe and a series of glimmering stone necklaces that reached past her waist. Her name badge bore the studio's logo in block letters. She had not seen my roommate in ten years, and the reservation was under my name, so the only one shuddering was my roommate. I figured it was the general air of edification.

A hidden speaker played thunderstorm sounds mixed with pan flute cascades. My roommate breathed into a brochure on reflexology. I asked the fortune teller if contact dermatitis was traceable via the spirit world, and if so, whether I had brushed up against something evil.

Hang on to Your Roommate

After a high school senior year "fun brawl" I realized how easy it would be to lose a tooth. Never fought unprovoked again. If I felt the urge to shove a stranger in the back at the movies, I did not. Punch a catcaller in the face? No way—I loved the attention, regardless of who was whistling *hot mama*. Flash forward, and my grad school roommate had signed us both up for SafetyZone training, early on a Monday morning. I wanted to slap the informational pamphlets to the floor, punt a cruller across the room, but resisted.

The organizers divided us into groups named *offense* and *defense*, and I didn't demand to be reassigned. Sat in my chair with hands folded in lap, concealing a fuzzy eraser shaped like a piece of Swiss cheese. Halfway through the session, I realized my roommate had earned five bucks per attendee recruited. How this was feasible with our prehistoric accounts payable office, who knows.

Once, at Key Bank, a stranger wiped out my entire savings with a counter check of accidental numbers. I lived alone then, and took my softball bat to the forest in anger. Only I dropped it alongside the train tracks before even getting to the trees. I suppose that's where my mind was when a training organizer told me to fix my posture. Suggested that I looked less than smart. In the old days, I might have punched right through a grave. My roommate raised one eyebrow like a silent film actor who accidentally opened a barrel of crows.

Adventures of Mary Van Pelt

I don't know, *was* the short story about me? Delilah stormed out of workshop and our professor groaned, reached for his thermos of prosecco. Delilah returned to stuff pages one through twelve into the garbage can. The story was accidentally single spaced. A water stain spread across the south wall of the seminar room, a moldy island. Karl chased after Delilah.

I'd brought half a day-old yellow layer cake to class with me. Feather glanced at her violin case. That was the day Jill wore shades to workshop for the first time. It was early enough in the new year that I was still "trying." Black and white striped tights with garters, metal lunchbox purse, hair flat-ironed on all sides by my roommate, who could level anything.

Michael was fiddling with his unflavored Chapstick again. Good thing I'd decided against wearing my t-shirt with "Denouement" across the chest in gangbanger Old English script. The clock was permanently stuck at 8:05, but the second hand kept rotating in stabs.

A surge of worry when I realized we'd forgotten to detach the massive adhesive eyelashes that my roommate had been peddling along with unpasteurized dairy products and hemp rock candy. I was blinking uncontrollably as the professor launched into a musty sermon on the downsides of verisimilitude. I couldn't help but read the first paragraph of my story again, albeit upside down.

Is it possible to be the heroine, and the villain, in your own work of fiction, but unintentionally? Bob was our closest thing to a creative nonfiction writer and attended class so infrequently that we joked he wasn't even real. The lights flickered a little. Suzanne coaxed open her bento box of snap peas, but the entire thing erupted like a canned snake, and Charlie screamed. Since Twitter would not be invented for another eight years, at that very moment Delilah sat in the computer lounge drafting a listserv manifesto about thinly veiled autobiographies masquerading as literary fiction.

That Stuff is Going to Kill You

Nothing is happening, I said to my roommate, who was speaking a series of letters and numbers into the phone. I walked to the window. Pulled an armful of paired socks out of the stacker bin. Looked at my fingernails and then glanced at my roommate, who crossed a name off a lengthy roster printed on dot matrix paper. *Should I take two*, I asked my roommate, who was cupping a hand over the receiver and making sounds that might have been in German.

It was mid-October. Earlier that day we had tried building a lion-noise box. Our Halloween costume longlist was workshopped across the entire kitchen whiteboard. Several of my premium oatmeal-colored undershirts mysteriously vanished into a wooden crate packed with stretched rubber and metal jacks. Our rejected costume ideas: Sid and Nancy, the Statue of Liberty and Ellis Island, a bowl of rotten pears, Dora Carrington and Lytton Strachey, two elk fleeing the same hunter. *How long has it been*, I asked my roommate while standing in front of the living room clock, the one I yearned to vivisect with my tweezer kit. Beneath the clock's face, a porcelain couple in white was sentenced to death every hour on the hour.

Remember that this was before you could purchase a quality keyboard for under $100, the kind that could play "The Monster Mash" using various keys of lion roar or groan. *My pupils are itchy*, I told my roommate, who was poised mid-dial on the rotary, sipping something beige with a fat straw. I decided to wash my feet, wanted everyone to know. Forgot that the bathtub was harboring the nascent lion-noise box, which trembled beside my toes and the sea-vomit of Victoria's Secret bubble bath. *I'm okay*, I shouted over the battery sizzle, past the amorous vinyl shower curtain, beyond the looming death knell of the porcelain couple at the strike of noon, into the ear of no one in particular.

The One Where We Explain "Mock Rock" to Our Lit Crit Professor

I made the sexiest Axl Rose back in 1990. On the night of the mock rock competition, girls and boys alike fawned over me before I even took the stage. The most popular kids at camp touched my hair unironically. Friends from back home—all of us rising juniors—rolled their eyes because I was always grinding to radio metal and whipping my head around and this was nothing new.

My roommate's mock rock experience wasn't part of teen discovery camp. It wasn't adjacent to a bake sale fundraiser where the loneliest girls prayed someone would bid on their banana nut muffins. "Imagine the Parisian arcades," my roommate begins, "but with only one spectacle." We're talking about Walter Benjamin in our lit crit class, so the professor remains engaged until my roommate recites a set list of Chemical Brothers and Underworld songs. I wonder aloud how anyone can lip sync to that music. Would the mock rockers inhabit thumps of bass with their shoulders? Sing the lyrics through aluminum foil?

My roommate gestures for the chalk and begins an elaborate sketch on the blackboard. I resume listing items tossed onstage that night when I careened to "Rocket Queen," penultimate track of the set. My favorite was a sole fingerless leather glove that plopped at my feet like a stray liver. Of course, I jammed my fist into it as I imagined Axl Rose would have done. Some of the suburban kids had clearly never beheld star power before. One teen (who looked familiar from spelling bee regionals) threw his glasses on the ground and attempted to tear open his polo shirt.

Finally, my roommate's blackboard sketch is complete. It looks like one of those mind's eye puzzles but without extra dimensions, or a knockoff M.C. Escher poster on sale in a mall kiosk. Our professor blanches like it's some kind of sinister talisman. He doesn't understand the concept of mock rock any better than he did thirty minutes prior.

The Slut-Scare Factor

My roommate exited the fitting room wearing a tank top with a microphone silkscreened across the chest. From a distance, it didn't look like a microphone. It was the day I first remember having lower back pain. October, but summery. I could still walk in stilettos, but only wore them to academic conferences, for the slut-scare factor.

Every year my roommate was invited to serve on an unrealistic number of panels. Even though I was still under twenty-five, my roommate insisted on massaging my scowl spot nightly. I felt like a bad pear. The only conference panels I served on were ones I chaired, only attended by my academic exes (who afterwards piled into one-seater bathrooms at noodle shops and rammed each other while talking about me).

On a hanger, the tank top looked like a garment you would be forced to wear selling snow-cones at a theme park. Quantifying my lower back pain for the specialist, I pointed at a line drawing of three bear cubs in an abandoned Volkswagen. My roommate paired that tank top with skinny pinstripe trousers, before they were in vogue.

The academic exes formulated questions that were more like comments about back pain as a symptom of guilt, felt handfuls of each other's armpit hair and left fingernail marks on the complimentary starlight mints. From the back of the ballroom, I regarded the glittery wind muff on my roommate's tank top, as the projector dropped slide after slide of unfiltered light.

Annual Proceedings

My academic exes slithered the conference book fair kissing cheeks of acquaintances, kissing cheeks of wine vendors, kissing security officers with adhesive credentials, kissing recently published scholarly monographs, kissing their own fingers, daydreaming about kissing the badges of favorite public intellectuals.

My roommate was straightening the seams on my black stockings when one academic ex lifted a trick water pitcher, the kind without a real bottom. I carried one of those leather lunchbox purses. My haircut was called "the widget," and outgrown, but still stylish. I always ate orange slices for breakfast, and though my roommate jogged the entire galleria seeking fresh fruit, we ended up with Tang and oyster crackers. Passed a paper cup of espresso brewed jailhouse style with a series of manipulated paper clips.

Some academic exes—maybe Finn, Kolby, and Shane—rushed to the aid of the ice water victim, while others sketched the scene on discreet Moleskines. Or maybe they were actually drawing me, draped across the cocktail stool like a weird piece of cloth. One of the organizers designed a frilled apron printed with conference logo and sample pages from the full program, but the price was prohibitive, even for my roommate, who hoarded travel funds like some grandmothers stockpile peppermint lifesavers or mysterious black and yellow caplets with no manufacturer stamp.

One lone academic ex breezed past wearing a t-shirt emblazoned with *Complacencies of the Peignoir* in glittery blue letters. A security officer radioed for more paper towels and then solicited my roommate to DJ the corporate dance party scheduled at dusk in ballroom three. I kept attempting to compose a joke about academic exes and fake pitcher bottoms.

Battle of Little Italy

My roommate follows my boyfriend down an alley, and it isn't pretty. Actually, both of them are quite pretty, but please don't tell them I said that. There's undue competition. My roommate stacks the bar jukebox with do-me-wrong songs, leaves the alcohol out of my alcohol. Angry-irons pleats into my work pants. Conducts research on bath bombs that cause urinary tract infections (so I can avoid them), and research on my boyfriend's whereabouts at a funeral with his wife (but not for his wife).

Do not question my roommate's intentions, which exceed the weak gestures of my parents, who created me as yet another bucket of experimental horticulture that didn't live up to the promises of the packet. My boyfriend is a self-taught craftsman, my roommate a doctoral candidate in aesthetics. One of the two was starting quarterback in high school. One of the two won a blue ribbon for a potato-battery clock at the age of five. It doesn't matter this July night in little Italy, as the lyric poets carve a square out of the narrative poets in the parking lot of the disappeared Rigby Homes project.

When a few ladies in leather pass by, it's my roommate that they commend me on, and noise of the brawl leaks through the Italian-style front windows. When the police arrive, they're the junior police, armed with slim pen flashlights. I explain to them that a boyfriend is replaceable, just like a pair of black polyester trousers.

The One Where We Write a Pilot for a Horror Drama about Roommates

We argue for forty minutes over who will be listed as "roommate A" and "roommate B" in notes for the script.

My roommate's last name begins with A.

Of course, this horror drama isn't about us. It's a work of fiction.

When I was a child the neighborhood kids often played *Little House on the Prairie*, and I wanted to be Laura due to my braids and sunny attitude but always had to be Mary because my name is Mary and never recovered from this injustice.

My roommate's creativity is tied to Carole King's *Tapestry* on vinyl, which I declare a cliché, but turn the volume up when asked.

Was the weather hideously balmy that day, making us traitors for staying indoors hashing out dialogue on legal pads? Which of my boyfriends was reclining on a futon on the other side of the living room wall?

Is it wrong that I can't recall either of these details, but remember exactly what my roommate was wearing? [Sherbet orange terrycloth shorts, long-sleeve navy t-shirt with "West Side Saints" in unreadable script, clear jelly sandals, a plastic bead bracelet that made as much noise as a blender.]

Once we have two pages of handwritten notes, my roommate suggests we switch the setting from a gutted post-industrial Midwestern town to a post-industrial Midwestern university stacked with angelic graduate students who look ready to kill and be killed.

I mix a pitcher of pink grapefruit Crystal Light, serve it over novelty ice cubes (boob-shaped, it was the 90s, we were crude back then) in plastic tumblers.

[Ten years after this pilot drafting session, one of my graduate students will tell me how to use Crystal Light powder to make intense flavored liquor, an epiphany one decade too late.]

My roommate is a vegan so nobody in the pilot bites anyone.

No suggestion of animals in peril, despite a few symbolic allusions to ecological demise.

Roommate A: It's so hot here in the seminar room. I miss our apartment's lake breeze.

Roommate B: We'll be home soon enough, Laura. Please put your Palm Pilot and gummi stars away.

Roommate A: I do not feel like being murdered by a ghost in a satin jumpsuit.

Halfway through the writing session our landlord, Dino, phones to tell us the water will be shut off for two to six hours. We fill the bathtub and kitchen sink and close all windows to prevent evaporation.

Against my better judgment I mention that we've never had a tornado warning in this building. Where are you supposed to go when you live on the tenth floor of a vintage mid-rise?

My roommate once wrote an anonymous *Chicago Reader* op-ed about the cheap ball point pens distributed to us by the graduate college. I thought they were nice, only a bit smudgy.

[It takes months for my students to finally convince me to watch *Yellowjackets*. I refuse initially, thinking it's yet another boring nature documentary.]

Neither of us are adept at plotting. We know this already. Once when we were both up for workshop someone entered the classroom before class and wrote "non-sequitur central" on the board in chunky graffiti-type block letters.

[Driving each of the Assistant Professor of Film Studies job finalists to Cleveland Hopkins airport in 2015, I recuse myself from answering any questions about my history in the scriptwriting discipline. *Just a member of the search committee who happens to have a clean Toyota Corolla*, I explain.]

After any brainstorm my roommate types up minutes, even if just a list of things we should be on the lookout for at TJ Maxx or Filene's Basement.

Appendix A: satin jumpsuit, fingerless mittens (lace), backpacks with sword-holders.

Sweat Equity

One day my roommate left the house in a black cotton tank and returned in a madras oxford that smelled of a stranger's armpits. The agency where we both summer-temped was wallpapered with headshots in various stages of "making it," the most famous of them autographed with Sharpie. I wanted to make it just like all the other iterations of myself, but my roommate claimed that notoriety was forged solely through sweat equity.

How long before any of us, wearing high-cut leotards under our saggy office khakis, would belong to anything resembling a *guild*? My roommate tried to open the apartment door with the laundry room key, then lurched forward, unleashing an armful of Cara Cara oranges. This was back when fruit merchants approached you at every stoplight, along with rag-rose sellers and free advice peddlers. My roommate could never resist.

We barely had the internet, but I still yearned to be message-board-famous and invented what I believed to be a new kind of plastic choker necklace. My latest temp assignment had me operating a switchboard while squatting between two desks. In the evenings I stretched my biceps as if fame waited on the other side of the mirrored closet. A clatter in the hallway: my roommate attempting to kick off a new pair of goat-leg stilts.

More Harm Than Good

The night before my roommate's appointment we taped an anatomical diagram of the head and neck onto the dartboard at Flounder's and just went at it. We knew so little about legitimate rituals back then. I accidentally left a piece of black tourmaline in my lunch sack overnight and then the next day the toaster broke, but I'm not sure those things were related.

We'd spent the whole day ironing out my roommate's identification card for student health services and then subjecting it to the traumas of the laminator in an effort to make things appear more official. Needless to say, my roommate was listless and agitated and couldn't partake in any self-medication aside from a transcendental meditation cassette and some eucalyptus-infused tube socks. I read aloud from an Erica Jong book I had never returned to the library, but that made things worse.

An article in *Sassy* once described how some people are most comfortable in the role of caretaker and will therefore wilt when having to assume the role of patient. Or maybe that was a research piece from *Eighteenth-Century Studies*. I began to wonder if my roommate's spirits would be lifted if I demonstrated unfortunate behavior, such as hyperventilating upon discovering a water bug in my bra, or downing a caplet handed to me by a man dancing his marionettes to Boz Scaggs on the corner.

This was before we had what is today known as a sheet mask, and people got high on things other than bath salts, so instead I staged a tableau vivant of *The Death of Marat* where Marat was actually a doctoral student in a nude leotard covered with shaving cream and sick in the bathtub from Mountain Dew sours, which I still avoid.

Nowadays, when addressing groups of prospective graduate students, I always close with this advice: find yourself a roommate strong enough to lift you from the depths of your worst idea. *What is a node, anyway?* I had written on the side of the bathtub in cherry Chapstick, but I'm uncertain if the message was ever delivered.

Late August Edition

Kids today have no idea what a thrill it was to flop the JCPenney catalog open on a lap and peruse both the toys and the fashions intended for back to school, even if nothing would meet the dress code's rigid standards. My roommate's dissertation began with one such statement, followed by action sculpture involving decommissioned fluorescent bulbs and handfuls of confectioner's sugar representing the after-product of tears.

I recalled how *Seventeen* magazine convinced me I would turn heads in blue mascara. My boyfriend claimed no memory of back to school or riding the bus to school or sitting in a classroom, only the hours he spent standing in a cinderblock smoking shanty getting rained on and feeling something weird on his tongue. With this information my roommate blanched and returned to a typewritten tract about how memories are an indication of depth, and certain case studies are as fruitful as a shoebox filled with cedar shavings.

I remembered my friend Starla who shoplifted so many items it was like watching a tumbleweed romance a littered fairground. At the fair, my charge was to sell raffle tickets using any means necessary, including spitting, intimidation, flagrant catcalls. After I dispensed their change, the men got right back in line. It was late August and excitement was limited.

My roommate's dissertation included a multimodal component where I was asked to pee on an upholstered wing chair. Even after a quart of Hawaiian Punch I was unable to perform. Of course, the chair represented unresolved friction with the bourgeoisie. My boyfriend claimed that the first time he set his wallet on fire it was an accident, and after that he realized he liked it.

My Romantic Period

Six months before I met my roommate I got lost in a shooting field outside London. British boots are made to withstand elements, including downpour and stumbling. I had red hair and was basically unrecognizable, except for the noncommittal almost-charcoal eyeshadow. Later my roommate would call this my Romantic period, but with slight jealousy, given the top-tier woolens I accumulated.

The host family wanted to keep me, but immigration said no. In my third-floor bedroom, I memorized the wallpaper of hedgerows and Victorian picnic baskets, attempted a few embarrassing sketches of my temporary mother. The shooting field swept along train tracks into the city. People say that Brits are extremely formal but there was no formality between marshy gravel and tagged sheds. My temporary mother looked like Virginia Woolf in profile, a fact that my roommate teased me about when we'd had too many amaretto sours at Flounder's.

One week before departure, the whole family (even Pear the cat, in a discreet floral carrier bag) journeyed to the city for a pub dinner. Then my host brothers surprised me with a trip to Wicked Haven for dancing and liquor, my temporary mother penning liner wings on my eyes right there at the table.

At this point in the story my roommate would interrupt and ask if I had perhaps crossed paths with Underworld, or whether Wicked Haven really lit the dance floor with the glow of furious electric eels. Then I would change the subject to *Trainspotting*, and how I saw a Mark Renton lookalike in O'Hare, kicking a paper cup around the baggage claim as I pulled my orange vinyl suitcase off the belt.

The Problem of Summer

My roommate never mourned a semester's death, just banished teaching blazers and swabbed every piece of a stolen office phone with rubbing alcohol. We had seventy-two hours between final grade submission and full-time employment as office temps, clerks, or bouncers, or working the translation hotline, which took me beyond the comfort zone of my French. Twelve hours to leave the bottom page of the grade triplicate form on the dining room table before filing it with takeout menus. Utility bills roiled like a haphazard crock pot stew.

Days earlier, students lined the hall outside my office fetching portfolios, sharing sticky blue candy and unicorn erasers, occasionally a mixtape or melon-scented candle. Afterwards I cried into my hair in the elevator. Looked at the sky and the sky gave me the finger. Blocks away, corporations awaited a new receptionist to really mix things up, someone with an eye for organization who was also an eyeful. At home, my roommate answered the phone with an inscrutable patois. Long-distance callers debated myriad connotations of the word *stalk*.

We had the luxury of two phone lines in our apartment, but the ring sounded the same for both. The phone instruction booklet was green and saddle-stitched, relic of a bygone era. Every button had only one purpose. Nowadays we might call it *midcentury chic*. Our apartment was too hot for fans, not hot enough for the rattling air conditioner that dangled from a window like a drunk tourist. Calls shuddered through the night in six different languages, and even with the ringer turned down I woke every time my roommate picked up.

Some of my friends were married and got to spend summers on a front porch with a pitcher of lemonade, wearing skirts for comfort rather than tips. Certain boyfriends tended other people's high-end teardowns, sipping Rolling Rock in the bathroom. A nemesis of yesteryear penned a casual memoir about a yacht named *The Debbie Gibson*. My roommate slipped one verb conjugation cheat book into another. Neither of us considered solving the problem of summer with a one-way train ticket or a rich old man.

The One Where We Find Our Way Out of a Pickle

It started like any ordinary Thursday afternoon, doing ordinary Thursday chores. But the washing machine cycle had been running for three hours and counting. Just when I thought it would make its final spin, the hoses kicked back on and the metal box flooded like a storm sewer.

My roommate was perched on a counter intended for folding towels. Our building's laundry room doubled as a workout room and had intersecting mirrored walls, which made us appear infinite. Near the doorway, someone had left one of those rolling metal baskets with the hanging garment bar. It certainly wasn't the management, which was known for limiting luxuries.

I started to get that panicked feeling like when I was at the end of a good novel. Locked inside Speed Queen #3, my favorite flannel rinsed again and again next to my roommate's work polo. In the buttoned pocket of that flannel: my set of apartment keys. Though my roommate wore a chain wallet with a studded key ring, it was only for fashion. We both needed to get back inside the apartment. My roommate needed a polo to wear to the night's shift at Video Heaven.

Our building management did not apply a "maximum lockout penalty policy" to the elderly renters who dropped their keys into a cup of morning coffee or ended up on the roof instead of in the lobby. But we had exhausted management's patience with the Great Purse Loss of February 1999, followed by the Great Pocket Hole Caper of March 1999. We knew better than to ask for Dino to dig out the sub-master.

Facebook was not yet invented, so we could not poll the toxic Our Old Apartment group about the likelihood that a door transom would be workable after decades of paint. Even if we were able to open it, could we actually shimmy through? We found one of those round library stools on the loading dock and shuttled it to the service elevator. A worker with a comically large dangling key ring stepped in behind us, like some kind of omen.

"Where are you headed?" my roommate asked, making a pouty face for no reason.

The man said something in German. I thought it was about reglazing a bathtub on the fifth floor. I tried to put my foot on the round stool, casual-like, to make it seem less awkward, but instead kicked it across the elevator with a clatter.

The man got off the elevator at five, gave us a quick nod.

In a sitcom version of this encounter, my roommate would produce the man's resplendent key chain as soon as the door closed, then we would scream with glee, jump up and down (which would feel weird in the elevator, but whatever) and then unlock our apartment. We were both starving. It was time for our cat's thyroid medication. My roommate could locate the backup work polo, which was acceptable even if pit-stained.

But this was not a sitcom, and my roommate wasn't that skillful with sleight of hand. We rolled the library stool to our door, and on tiptoes my roommate could put fingertips on the transom. Down the hall, someone was listening to The Loop-Chicago's Classic Rock on the radio, blasting "Jamie's Cryin'."

When we'd first toured the place, Dino had told us about the building's vaudeville history, stopping short at the part where morals were so loose that moans of ecstasy issued out of doorway transoms day and night, occasioning their eventual closure. One group of residents petitioned to stop the noise, while another petitioned to keep the breeze.

Of course, our transom wouldn't budge.

As my roommate attempted to pick the door lock instead, I took the elevator back downstairs and grabbed the rolling basket from the laundry room. Would we use it as a battering ram? Tent it with a tarp and camp under it until we figured out how to get back in? I was near tears when the elevator stopped at the fifth floor. The man with the glorious keychain clattered back on. Dialects of my childhood neighborhood boiled in my throat.

In improvised, imprecise German, I told him that I was a stupid, humble maid. My employer's panties were trapped in the washing machine that was running eternal! I had locked myself out and needed the key to the castle.

The man did not yield the keychain. He might not have understood much of what I tried to say in German. I acted out the plight of the washing machine, realizing that I looked like a stand mixer churning batter. Reversing course, I pantomimed hanging laundry on a line.

It took approximately thirty seconds for him to halt the Speed Queen. It paused a few seconds, lights flashing, and then unlocked.

As my flannel and my roommate's polo tumbled in the dryer, we fried up some turkey bologna for the man, told him about our cat's thyroid struggles, and played him some obscure German electronica on vinyl.

Penguin Classics Edition

One night we ate questionable ferns and my roommate kept back-tracking *Pet Sounds* to "That's Not Me." A literary protagonist from our summer reading list was languishing in the wasteland of her misogynistic author's fantasy forest. After a visit to the food co-op, we were poised to join her odyssey with our own abundance of fiddleheads.

Were we supposed to cook the fiddleheads first, weep them, de-fang them? The rest of the night was blank. Every turn of the ceiling fan felt like a sword-swoop. Some woman was brushing her hair in our bathroom and neither of us knew her, but we didn't want to be rude. Which of us invited her over? Was it because she faintly resembled the painting of the novel's protagonist as displayed on the cover of the Penguin Classics edition? Did she work at the fiddlehead food co-op, and had we asked her home to partake?

We had no choice but to play it cool. Remember, this was before the internet was a big deal, so we couldn't just search images of which ferns were appropriate for consumption. At some point one of us got into an argument with the woman about the complex merits of *Trainspotting*. My roommate typically spent six hours every day at a typewriter with a burning Newport, producing zero words per minute, but we did not mention this to the woman as she described the French braids she favored as a young girl in Milwaukee.

I had a habit of getting *really into* my favorite novels, including cosplay and unwise injury reenactments. Even while hallucinating and terrified of the shower curtain, I managed to quote vast tracts of the novel by heart, and it seemed like the woman was impressed. My roommate indulged me, then enabled me, sponging the fern bits off my legs.

At some point we must have poured the woman a bowl of generic corn flakes. It dawned on us that someone should walk the woman home, but we had no idea where we had found her, or if she was even real. My roommate eased back at the typewriter but was not at ease. I asked the woman to play the role of the protagonist's wretched boss in a hat factory. I would align myself on the floor like a misplaced spangle.

Blood and Moss (in my roommate's voice)

Chicago, 2:24 am
To Whom It May Concern: It's hard to say when the trouble began, but trouble is a flawed term. Purchasing a power washer seems the solution to most stains yet proves useless for all but blood and moss. If granted this literary arts residency fellowship I, Mary Van Pelt, will continue to produce the highest quality work, the art that makes you welcome ants beneath your most tender garments, or offer your tongue to the nearest demolition site.

And what is my work? Consider the last time you vomited more than twice in one hour. What were your thoughts like? Probably dreamscapes much aligned with the enclosed poem "Man in My Mother's Coat," pinning a fever-pitch to a cock crow under the throbbing lights of the House of Busirane, which is a reference to *The Faerie Queene*, not among the clubs I've danced in over the past decade, at some points riotously underage.

But the troubles piled up nonetheless and I couldn't grind them away with a flick of the figurative tail. To wit: my favorite boyfriend is leaving for Italy with his wife and there's talk of an impending conception and purchase of real property. The only things keeping me docked in the harbor: my art, and to a much less tumultuous degree, my roommate, who is the father and mother I never had, being raised on a strict diet of observable outcomes and tiered facts.

Be assured that if issued a fellowship for this residency I will arrive outfitted in bespoke garb appropriate for a high-caliber country estate. The aforementioned roommate, a hybrid of humble nurse and devoted valet, has prepared the enclosed ("colour") plates as a rendering of my various sartorial possibilities.

At this point it would perhaps be appropriate to mention I've been published in *Ploughshares*, a fact only my loyal champion-roommate celebrated by hiring a helicopter and purchasing airtime for a vanity interview on National Public Radio. Do not bother perusing the attached writing sample for a poem in which my favorite boyfriend surprises me with six dozen ice roses and a cake with the first five stanzas of "Winter Veins" etched in marzipan, because it never happened, and while one should not conflate the speaker of a poem with its author, my poems seethe with verisimilitude, much like the drips of spray-flock my roommate uses on our dance cages to encourage holiday-caliber tips.

The night in Greektown when my favorite boyfriend posited that my cat loved him more, and that she would gladly crawl into his bag and return home to the ranch with its yeast-white carpets, I stormed home and even the street lechers were alarmed by my visage. Sometimes I become so furious that every muscle in my face twitches, as if I'm already a worm-wearing vessel. But when I looked through the dangling bead curtain—its shivers a trademark of our home's aesthetic—and regarded my serene roommate reading aloud from *The House of Mirth* to our wee tabby Pandora, a plate of disassembled sushi nearby, my ire calmed and I settled down at the typewriter where I am now penning this statement of purpose, which I enclose in a handmade envelope, on paper woven from premium imported linens, much like those I might sport stepping off the train with my steamer trunk and smart bonnet.

A Willing Participant

My roommate was painting my toenails black while eating an orange ice lolly. You have to remember that technically we lived on the beach, even if our nearest shore was all rocks. Sorority types played sand volleyball elsewhere. Our beach was mostly lone men in London Fog raincoats, stray hounds, and deceased minnows riding the wake.

My roommate was applying an eyebrow masque on both of us, but only one of us was a willing participant. I posited that the apartment would look more sacred with stained glass and enhanced statuary. My roommate suggested that I should phone manager Beth at Flounders and ask for more shifts.

We could see a storm system in the distance, or maybe that was just the fuzz on the horizon that we called "Indiana." This was long before anyone considered doctoral programs in English or Aesthetics to be frivolous, unlike Law, which would have put us in boxy suits consuming mustard sandwiches at midnight.

Since we had no Amazon.com account back then, my roommate had purchased a henna kit from the head shop and was perplexed by the instructions. In hindsight, I realize that we were both thinking about how we had friends who died that winter. Would my roommate mold me into "the next Shane," even if unintentionally? How many times could I tap out of a cocktail party claiming grief? The henna kit had few patterns and over ten steps.

My roommate was making some practice sketches of a crow wearing heart-shaped sunglasses. I preferred my epiphanies gentle. One morning that summer I woke to find my roommate had painted a trompe l'oeil fireplace on the wall. The fire licked its own leg like a cat.

American Migraine

All I remember about that semester was the pair of burgundy velour track pants my roommate brought home when I was crying over my workload. I had no idea where the pants came from, as the label appeared to be in Sanskrit, and there was no trace of price tags or packaging. My roommate had cleverly knotted the pants in a few spots, giving the impression of a deflated balloon animal.

At the time I was wearing my usual migraine pants: blue stripes, too short and pajama-ish to wear in public. We turned all three of our HEPA filters on and the lake slapped beach rocks like a catfight. I was procrastinating about grading papers. This, you see, has never changed. Back then I would do literally anything but start them: calling random businesses in the phone book, attempting to fast-clone clips of our house plants, inventing new card games, badgering the reference librarian. My roommate had purchased an angel statue that looked just like me, and that was supposed to be motivational, but instead smacked of lost innocence.

We put some ginger oil on the back of my neck. Of course, this was prior to the mainstream essential oil boon. We attempted my distant Polish granny's migraine remedy which asked us to identify a tree, beg it for a tooth, and then bury the tooth at the foot of the tree. I had four Hawaiian Punch toddies under my belt and kept toppling over but blamed it on the sugar content. My roommate could power through a stack of fifty papers in forty minutes on the elliptical stepper. Finally, I traded my old migraine pants for the new migraine pants, which were like stepping into a parcel of velvet blood.

Butterscotch Schnapps & Dead Air

If my roommate ordered a buttery nipple shot and queued "Smooth Operator" on the jukebox, we were in for a long night. I took too much time in the library map room, trying to be discreet measuring distances. Chicago to Pittsburgh. Chicago to Copenhagen. Copenhagen to the middle of the ocean, where someone had attempted a math problem in pencil.

If my roommate put on silver sequined shorts on a non-teaching day. If morning haze never quite peeled back, the #8 Halsted bus feeling less like an international sea vessel and more like a paint can shaker. If all the best cafeteria sandwiches were sold out or expired, and my roommate only stashed one can of emergency pineapple SlimFast for both of us. If my roommate suggested we practice our telepathy, since one of us would inevitably end up a ghost. Handful of pencils on the table between us, stack of scratch paper repurposed from a *Shakespeare Quips* calendar, ungraded student essays about remembering events.

After our last class on Thursdays, we would go home and watch a morbid thriller, eat a snack mix of pepitas, carob chips, pretzel goldfish, and red pepper flakes. My roommate might pretend to doze until the minute I touched the remote. If the answering machine recorded several minutes of dead air for every screened call. If I was the first one to suggest heading to the bar. If I put on a slutty tank beneath an ordinary sweater, a ratty jacket. If I called my ex from a payphone while my roommate slammed a buttery nipple shot with the bartender. If I hung up before he answered.

Love Taker, Lease Breaker

My student shoves a novel off the edge of a desk. Nobody moves to pick it up, including me. The entire class in disbelief. Back in the 90s—era distant as the Bronze Age to this group—we used to randomly shack up. For example: Jason Fleming met Rose Schneider in workshop, leveled a few generous remarks on "digging deeper," and then moved his footlocker of sweaters into her studio. My friend Kelby crashed on her officemate's futon chair for eighteen months, leaving only when a new acquaintance offered a lofted twin bed with drawers underneath.

The protagonist of the novel (which now sits facedown near a puddle of boot-melt) yearns to make it in the music industry and is willing to sleep in a stranger's bathtub until this happens. Completely implausible to all students in the classroom, threatening mutiny.

Sure, we had trouble vetting connections back then, with no digital footprint to reference. At the grad school orientation mixer, my soon-to-be roommate cut across the dance floor like a runaway yacht. I tried counting the number of buckles on my future roommate's patent leather boots, got distracted by the elbow-length fishnet gloves.

I was in white denim booty shorts left over from undergrad, black knee socks and Mary Janes, a glittery cat face tee. My roommate carried a Miller Lite in one hand, Long Island in the other, as I ignored my watery amaretto sour. We had no idea the university's system would soon pair us together, index cards overlapping via Aquarius moon and academic discipline. We were just two people on a dance floor feeling both sentimental and ambivalent about Depeche Mode.

Is an apartment lease a covenant? Nobody judged when Rose traded Jason out for Ron, who only lasted until spring break. I didn't know my roommate well enough when we signed the triplicate form, so withheld an untoward remark about binding clauses. It only took three hours of milk crates, pizza rolls, and radio station browsing to become eternal confidantes.

Perhaps it was the moment I sneezed my left contact lens out and my roommate caught it and popped it back into my eye with one virtuosic swoop. We deferred to my roommate's taste in hair products, placed my spice collection in foreground of the rack. I vowed never to let any stupid hookups crash on our couch for more than six hours. My roommate promised to read all of my workshop story drafts without critique until the end.

My Roommate as Pastel Goth in Century Shopping Centre Elevator

You may not already know this, but I lived in Chicago as a small child and then left. My family relocated to a suburb where people built decks from decommissioned railroad ties and passed out Dixie cups of warm Hi-C. And then we fled Illinois altogether. So back in the city for grad school, when I mysteriously knew the numbers of all the buses my roommate thought I was either clairvoyant or full of shit. Tired of my stupid boyfriend and his club softball league, I hopped a series of trains without thinking and arrived at the correct stop. Even after accidentally eating two atomic hash brownies, I provided accurate directions to La Crêperie.

My roommate was completely new to Chicago but familiar with Midwestern metropolis as concept. Nary a junior high trip to the tourist traps, no lukewarm heap of mozzarella on stiff crust. *How can you make it to twenty-five without ever visiting Chicago?* I thought, as my roommate read a throwaway pamphlet about the SS *Eastland* disaster.

Maybe I took advantage from time to time—adding a layer of cryptozoology to the old water tower, implying that my grandfather saved countless souls from the Our Lady of the Angels inferno—but it was gentle hazing. My roommate devised a ghost-catcher from a clementine net but we rarely had it on hand when things got weird.

Decades later, I would evoke dim arcades of the atrophied Century Shopping Centre as a metaphor for mid-pandemic higher education and nobody would get it, which was typical. Even back in 1999, the tamest pleather Unlisted loafer issued a stomp in those voided corridors. Though it was the swan song of our lease—my roommate pondering co-ops, my nights split between equally lumpy beds of several dim boyfriends—we went to see *Jesus' Son* in the theater at Century as soon as it debuted. My roommate snuck in two bags of dehydrated apricots and a glass terrine of crème fraîche. Jim DeRogatis sat a few rows away from us, but we pretended not to notice. Afterwards we took the elevator all the way down to catacomb level, and my roommate spun to ambient mechanical noise in a bonnet-blue raincoat.

Too Much Charge

The new year loomed like a pair of torn pantyhose in a ditch. Neither of us wanted to touch it. My roommate kept flipping our Scarecrows of America calendar back to November. I couldn't reach the bin where we stored our cat's Baba Yaga costume. Somebody kept buzzing our apartment intercom looking for "Sheila."

My roommate had decorated the radiator covers for Christmas: cloven hooves trimmed out of spare felt, Dickensian waif silhouettes in charcoal. I was obsessed with a scratchy blue flannel even though it felt like aggressive dermatitis. It belonged to yet another ex-boyfriend, the one who relocated to Yellowknife because Chicago "lacked authenticity."

On our new year resolution roster, my roommate applied one glittery holographic sad face sticker to the category of *romance*. We killed a few hours roller skating in the utility room. The housekeepers laundering Victorian garments of ancient inhabitants of the top floor—left over from the building's vaudeville days—called us *hookers* in Polish. Half of my ancestors were straight out of Podlaskie Voivodeship, which I couldn't even pronounce, and I think the housekeepers could tell.

In 1986, a crime show film crew shooting in our apartment building released an accidental fireball that cascaded up to the twelfth floor, blowing doors off hinges and melting a few kitchens. *Too much charge*, the stunt master had claimed in a newspaper clipping. We reeled around a corner and down the half-flight of stairs, claiming to catch a shiver of ghost smoke left over from the inferno crew. My roommate shared an old trick of enveloping yourself in the nearest floor-length drapes, becoming virtually invisible. The housekeepers shuttled past us with their borax, curses, and bundled reeds.

Hysteria Pitch

My roommate knew how to refurbish a laptop using common tools from a makeup bag. Eyelash curler and slimmest tweezers, a couple of those horrid makeup sponge wedges, and a cast-off gloss roller. Yet none of this coaxed my beloved Gateway 2000 laptop to reboot.

It was early January, and my hysteria pitch had already exceeded its monthly allotment. Around noon I sobbed into our empty mailbox. A neighbor's cavy had recently fallen out the window. A favorite ex had lost a finger (my favorite finger) in a snowblower mishap. While I wept into a series of Jäger shots, a bar thief lifted my backpack filled with obscure interlibrary loan items. So when my roommate covered my face with a marabou duster and spun me around in a desk chair, my first thought was barfing. But there it was, computer resurrected and the internet launched, glittery purple animated letters spelling BABY GIRL in a banner.

My roommate was talking on two different phones, neither of which occupied the main line. An exchange about hot links, which I gathered were not the pork variety we craved after smoking a bowl. My roommate settled down at a table populated with three different antique typewriters. I blinked a few times then began entering text.

In Pre-Enlightened Times

We had the internet but only perused it for one hour on weekday afternoons. Students left messages with the department secretary, who transcribed the note onto a pink template pad. *Seth*, it said in cursive, *would like you to know that somebody made off with the library books on reserve*. By the time my roommate received that message, boot-cut jeans were no longer in fashion. *Seth*, the message continued, *wonders if a photocopy might be available*. For those who never rode the bus with a conspicuous pocket full of nickels for the copier: lucky you.

Once I had a boyfriend who worked at Kinkos and wore a knit hat all of the time, even in bed. My roommate called him the feed-bagger on account of the hat but was probably jealous. All of that boyfriend's messages were mysteriously zapped from the answering machine. Static electricity, faulty handsets, too-curly cords: all to blame. I took pride in the shabby ephemera of my graduate assistant office and its cat stickers. Occasionally I slept on the windowsill, wrapped in scarves left behind by grad students of yesteryear.

One day my roommate called my office phone from one floor below, asking if I had any Folger's crystals. I only had loose green tea. I was wearing a hideous pewter insect brooch. A pink note warning me to discontinue "optimizing" the department photocopier landed in my mail slot. Back at home, I argued with my roommate over which VHS tape was which (they all had the same tri-color sticker and no text). Applied a peel-off facial masque that was too thin to peel. Soaked all my black lace headbands in the bathroom sink at once.

Fashionable Gloom

Around 9:30 am the talent agency receptionist made it to the bottom of her clipboard and my number was up. Even if all they needed me for was a love scene extra, a couple of moans, or somebody to throw a coffee mug across the room and cry into a curtain, that meant a new line for the curriculum vitae.

It's ironic to think of my roommate as an instinctive stage mother, but years later, watching dance mom documentaries, I gasped. I loved showering in the temporary trailer after filming, as my roommate scrubbed a spray bronzer off my knees. This was before we had any term for "self-care," but my roommate could have invented it: fuzzy terrycloth robe, hot water bottle stuffed into a cheerful plush scarecrow, facial masque that smelled like horseradish and clove.

I recalled how my own mother sent me back onto the ice bleeding from knees and nose, tore out any loose strands of hair that didn't make it into my braids.

While I was on set, my roommate read a series of trashy French romance novels, alluding to dissertation research, but we both knew better. Every novel involved a fin de siècle actress experimenting with fashionable gloom.

At 9:35 am, the Broad on Broadway micro-agency rang for a restaurant scene. They were shooting at a diner around the corner from 203 North LaSalle, where I once worked as a receptionist. The showy junior executives sometimes brought back a dirty Bloody Mary to-go pitcher to share, joked that the club sandwiches were as heavy as clubs.

"Bring your own slut-wear," the receptionist said before hanging up.

Trick Ethics

For such an old hotel, the doors of the Sheridan Arms sure were flimsy. I thunked and thunked in borrowed platform boots. Down the street, workers and their sledgehammers pledged to make the artisanal cheese chateau more modern. I tried to touch nothing but found my fingerprints everywhere. My hands always felt greasy in 1999, whatever I was doing, swabbing a stray cat's ear mites or assembling a fake authentic vaudeville hatbox. Arranging dates with a fake boyfriend as cover for dates with an even more fake boyfriend, keeping my roommate in the double dark.

Some roommates are tragedy-proof. Know them by the cuffs of their khakis, the reliability with which they produce a minipack of tissues from an oxford pocket. My roommate never identified as tragedy-proof, and perhaps I did, but only on paper. Filling out the university housing survey had felt like a flashback to my old summer job at Clothestime, with all the trick ethics. If your roommate secrets a mock-pietà necklace retailing approximately $8.99 and returns it the next day, packaging intact, is that a crime and do you report? I nicked the backs of my hands with a tag-trimmer, stood in line for grilled cabbage at the end of my shift.

According to the *Tribune* archives, a total of seven people had been murdered at the Sheridan Arms, two on the same night, and this brought a chill. Which was the most hideous crime: taking off all your clothes in front of a semi-stranger and watching each item fall to the floor, stepping outside a hotel room door for one minute in nothing but bracelets too byzantine to remove, or inventing a story that involved both? Dishonesty with a roommate is like sitting down at the piano and playing a fake song, then claiming the lyrics are too provocative to sing.

Even the most stereotypical hotel neon evokes pounding Rolling Rock on an empty stomach while perched on a bar stool in denim booty shorts. Once inside the Sheridan Arms hotel room I opened a solitary bar of Dial like it was a freak condom. Peered across the alley at my apartment building, as if I was leaving one body at home while the other hovered in two inches of hot water. Meanwhile my roommate was underlining every sentence in a research article using fluorescent pink highlighter.

How long until my date was standing at the door whispering something original like *knock, knock*? The rubber gloves in my purse belonged to my roommate. Cherry Chapstick on my bottom lip belonged to my roommate. 250 square feet of almost-lake view belonged to me until exactly 5:00 pm EST. I commenced my ritual of peering under the bed, opening the closet, unfolding the ironing board that smelled like divorce and damp ribbons.

The First Day of Class

Staying up late inventing first-day icebreakers with my roommate. Sitting outside the juice shop that would be leveled by explosives a week later. Ordering weird shots from the red sauce Italian place next door (the "coup de grace," the "tie-die Prince Albert"). Opening all the mail we hadn't bothered opening that month. Pranking my ex-boyfriend from a heavily tagged payphone.

Riding in adjacent seats on the Red Line, gossiping across strangers. Looking with disinterest at a restaurant roof on fire. Recalling the time our train smoldered underground, the guy with the Taurus 85 in his waistband. Why did I have to wear my slutty gold zodiac t-shirt that day? Why did I still smell like a man I had washed off my body with borrowed Irish Spring three hours earlier?

By the time mid-semester rolled around, all the students knew my roommate, but we still played the innocent bystander prank: my roommate delivering an "audio visual cart" consisting of mop buckets and feathered halos and bags of dried beans. When I visited my roommate's classes I was usually bumming Pepto Bismol, hot with the shudders of another breakup, or attempting to tape together a broken flip flop.

The first day of class is always equal parts ice and hot, like a shaken Coca-Cola retrieved from the bottom of a backpack. Fashioning weird musical instruments and instructing the students to captain them. Sketching a permanent Sharpie troll village on the whiteboard. Ransacking a paper bag filled with various adhesive tails. Nowadays you could never get away with such icebreakers, especially the one where you have to trace your neighbor's hand.

Curator of the Year

It was a period of "laying low" after the pedagogy awards ceremony fiasco. I was still mortified after penning a mini-invective against the presumed winner, drinking two pitchers of beer (out of the pitcher), then unexpectedly winning and performing a revolting dance at the podium. But within the confines of my favorite Pottery Barn, which we frequented daily, I was simply another style curator.

Sometimes I finessed the merchandise into more positive angles. Polished the weekender spoons against my tank top. At the awards ceremony podium I could barely hold the novelty award check steady but still executed the *drop it low* as if no time had passed since undergrad. I tried to abandon this memory in a glass fishbowl filled with seashells.

One Pottery Barn sales associate lingered next to my roommate, who was pondering the cost-effectiveness of homemade rattan, and then fifteen minutes later that same clerk was perched on my roommate's knee talking about Swedish up-dos and pillows stuffed with alternative down. I was doing a great job of not thinking about the particulars, such as what kind of beer was in those pitchers (Miller Lite) and which jukebox songs I'd played on repeat to pump up my outrage before the awards ceremony.

After the ceremony my roommate hand-fed me dates and made guillotine gestures at the bartender, but I just kept railing on about Scott Fennell and his feckless pedagogy paper on passive assessment. At least I still had Pottery Barn, I thought, running through every retained fragment of dialogue from the post-awards reception, where my roommate claimed to be re-clasping my bracelet but actually tied my wrist to a railing.

Around 8:00 pm we needed to make a purchase before Pottery Barn closed. My roommate strolled to the cash register with an armful of wooden beads, a six pack of plastic lemons, and a perfumed drawer buddy. I (accidentally) slammed one tiny sweet dreams bar soap onto the counter.

The One Where We Trick Tourists into Learning How to Dance

I own three different tourist disguises, but the most convincing includes three layered tank tops, low-rise distressed jean shorts, and a straw hat with plastic feather in the brim. I whisk on silver-pink iridescent lipstick and grab my shell necklace and I'm ready to rock the plaza.

Historically the plaza was dominated by flamenco demonstrations and noncustodial fathers herding children to the cotton candy cart. The flamenco demonstration was equally compelling and off-putting. The dancers wanted nothing to do with onlookers. It made us feel like we'd walked in on a stranger who forgot to lock the bathroom stall.

My roommate purchases a performer permit template and ream of 20-pound paper from a guy named Eddie who has a tiny office on Clark. The bootleg template spits out of our living room printer and I endorse it with my finest bureaucratic flourish.

Of course we have to arrive at the plaza separately. My roommate brings the boom box, bag of marabou boas, and mini trophies purchased from the party store.

It pains me to pay for a taxi, but we need to maintain verisimilitude. I smile at the taxi driver and tell him yes, it's my first time in Chicago and I can't believe how big and clean it is.

My roommate convenes a modest crowd, the plaza sidewalk chalked with foot outlines like we stood on in junior high when learning the electric slide. The flamenco dancers are nowhere to be found. A few weeks later, a fifty-word diatribe will appear in the *Chicago Reader* regarding the loss of culture downtown.

I stop at the cotton candy cart and order two pink-and-blues.

My roommate works the crowd. Speaks into a microphone that isn't connected to anything but does not need amplification. *Are you ready to rock? Are you ready… to rock?*

A couple with matching Cubs jerseys ventures into the circle my roommate has drawn in glitter chalk. I set down my cotton candy and step in like a dorky cartoon rabbit.

"Have you ever danced before?" my roommate asks, tips the mic to my face.

"Um, just square dances back in my home in Iowa and whatnot," I say.

I follow my roommate's lead, align flipflops with the footprints. I'm clumsy at first as if dancing had been banned in my hometown and I only attempted it in a crawlspace under my family's split-level where I stashed a JCPenney catalog since its families looked so happy with their untangled dogs and unnaturally green lawns.

Then, as the kids say today, the beat drops.

I rip the straw hat from my head and fling it into the crowd, where a noncustodial dad catches it in his teeth. Peel off two of the three tanks, revealing a nude cami that matches my skin.

Almost everyone screams.

I slide my body across the plaza with sick delight, like a lava lamp cracked open and spilling forbidden contents.

My roommate shrieks with excitement as I writhe up the plaza stairs and whip my hair.

"From the cornfields of Iowa, can you imagine," my roommate exclaims, then passes my hat to the crowd, waves copies of a dance how-to pamphlet (printed on 20-pound paper) for sale. "Now she's ready to take her show to the finest nightclubs and boudoirs in the Midwest."

Afterwards we dump the contents of my hat onto the Bennigan's bar counter—mostly singles—and decide to split an order of seasoned fries.

Gift of the Roommate

You know the type: can't wait for Christmas, and even on Christmas can't wait for the next Christmas. Neither of us were like that. I always found presents strangely embarrassing. My roommate was more of a giver than a receiver, devoted more time to elaborate wrapping than I spent deliriously shopping in the aisles of Filene's Basement.

Afterwards I required a cinnamon roll and a cider but instantly regretted both and spent an hour on the Stairmaster. In the mirror I watched my roommate pair socks with unbridled fervor. I'd put a sweater in the dryer again. Basically unteachable. I stepped harder. Fell asleep in the bathtub and dropped my cherished hardback of *Anna Karenina* into the suds water. "Was it an autographed copy?" my stupid boyfriend asked, thankfully out of earshot, roommate juicing a particularly resistant handful of beets.

We estimated that 75% of our mutual friends would be giving or receiving engagement rings or other commitment tokens that Christmas. Flex commissioned a mini pair of nuptial handcuffs to surprise Gary with on Christmas Eve, or so my roommate claimed with disdain. Something about a helicopter ride, honey-dipped strawberries (*shouldn't that be chocolate or goat's milk*, I queried without response), a payphone handsomely bedazzled with stick-diamonds. My roommate paused to lift an ice cube from the bottom of my platform boot—I'd walked through tar and gum on the same afternoon and was not allowed on the carpet.

The next day was Christmas. I endured a feverish dream that was both Dickensian and flecked with subtext from *Lost Highway*. Woke to something hot and wet in the bed, but that was just me. A light shuddered at the base of our trompe l'oeil fireplace, forming a Tolstoy-shaped shadow. "For my roommate, on this Christmas and every Christmas," the inscription read in loopy glitter script.

Graduate College Exit Interview Response #7

What aspects of your graduate studies do you expect will be most helpful for your future career path?

It's still April, but the weather report is promising upper sixties, so we make cutoffs from our most ragged jeans and head to the beach. Neither of us brings something to read. I forget the sunscreen but it's the late 90s and we are under thirty so it doesn't matter.

We have nothing to read but have packed three different lunches: hardboiled eggs with salt and pepper and a baggie of hot sauce, leftover Nutella crêpes from a midnight street vendor, and half a vegan hero on stiff rye. We should be doing a hundred other things. My roommate's dissertation prospectus is twelve days overdue. I'm three assignments behind in grading. But the waves don't care, so cold they immobilize my ankles as I wade in.

My roommate has a tiny battery-operated radio and plays a pop hits station that we normally would mock, but on the beach in late April it feels right. When a horsefly lands on my back, my roommate shoos it before any damage is done. In fact, I don't even know that it lands there, because I'm asleep face-down on my sweatshirt. My roommate slips both of our wallets into a mesh beach bag for safekeeping then searches nearby bushes for scraps of newspaper that might still be readable after recent storms.

I've never been very good at sleeping. As an undergrad my friends would always wake me up in the middle of the night, stuff me into a PVC jumpsuit, rat my hair, and drive us all to a dance club across the Canadian border. Of course, this was back when you could get through customs with cleavage and a wink. My sleep cycle never recovered, so it's unusual that I'm completely zonked at the beach in late April. Normally I would be rolling through my mind-easing mantras, thoughts of calm rivers interrupted by worries about missed periods and degree clearance and obscure monographs disintegrating in my study carrel.

My roommate returns with a wrinkled sleeve of *Chicago Reader* missed connections. When I wake up we read it together, wondering if any of the chance encounters are about us. Maybe the missed connection titled "SEXY DUO, backpacks, knee socks, Halsted bus, want to write my paper (or more)." During the nap, my roommate has purchased cotton candy for each of us. The sand already smells like summer even though it's far away.

I have no idea that this is the last time I will ever relax, and it will be a complete accident. My roommate hums that stupid Sugar Ray song. Some teenage skaters in the distance lob a hacky sack at each other. With a piece of gnarled driftwood, I write the title of my dissertation in wet sand at the shore. My roommate and I both shriek when a wave washes every word away.

Green and Infinite

One Saturday morning in June, my roommate resolved to become a gardener and never looked back. We lived on the tenth floor of a vintage mid-rise. Our only tillable land: a potting soil mishap on the rooftop deck. My roommate wanted to see the sky through the eyes of something green and infinite. That was the summer I started compulsively watching childbirth television shows, which fueled hasty breakups and cabbage soup diets.

My favorite childbirth show episode featured a couple who built their own live-in terrarium. The celebrity host avoided the subject of where a baby would sleep. Complaints from neighbors, jokes about glass houses, the wife shaking a French braid out of her hair. My roommate once made me take a pregnancy test before I sampled ceviche we concocted without a recipe. Our farm-share basket included leeks that looked like monster body parts.

My roommate exited the apartment and returned an hour later with several bags from Vintage Swap: overalls, knee-savers, gloves optimized for falconry but also suitable for prairie work. I was still in my booty-short pajamas with "Lady" written across the ass in barely readable pink bubble letters. One of our cats dragged a wide-brimmed straw bonnet from a bag, the other toothed a pink ribbon. I tried to locate sunscreen, only found Blistex.

We rode the escalator up to the gardening section in Borders, tote conspicuously filled with bok choy seeds and Miracle Gro. My roommate breezed fingers through an artificial money tree on the landing. I had applied so much natural mosquito repellant—fragranced like Pine Sol and Dreft—that I looked ready to slide across the bar at Flounder's. The old country kerchief slipped off my head and got stuck in the escalator's teeth.

Spin of the Randomizer

One Friday night—splitting an order of steak frites at Café Colette, seated in the heavy smoker section of the patio—my roommate tore a small hole in our narrative. What if the randomizer had made one more rotation? Phone numbers dropped into a spinner at the roommate matchmaking event, fished out by a different stranger's hand. I could have been commuting to campus from a rustic cabin on Lake Ass, my roommate shacked downtown with an engineer who owned stainless steel couches. We laughed it off, but later I felt nauseous getting out of the shower.

My alternate reality roommate had rich parents who rented out the cabin for five bucks a month just to keep the rugs clean. My roommate's engineer owned three socket wrench sets and never replaced the fridge water filter. In some bizarre reversal, we imagined those two alternates ended up roommates, splitting time between the chilly pied-à-terre and exurban country brambles, socket wrench sets rattling together like pill bottles in the trunk. Perhaps they were both gigantic babies when they got splinters walking barefoot on the pier, requiring a third party to intervene.

Our actual apartment was close enough to the shore to view a crack of Lake Michigan from the bedroom. An unseen vessel issued a plaintive ship-sound again and again into the dark. A booze cruise, lost fishing boat, floating ghost. At that moment, our alternate reality friends unboxed an assortment of champagne flutes, spread Laughing

Cow cheese on water crackers. I fell into frantic thoughts like a goat on slick sidewalk: boxes of disassembled bookcases and end tables, each requiring its own discrete wrench. On the opposite side of the room divider, my roommate dreamed of burying a disco ball on a beach.

Late Summer of 1999

All we could think about was rituals. My roommate hyperaware of splendor levels. A sequin to my grommet. First cat paw on a face after collapsing on the couch. Someone down the hall listening to Filter at dawn. A ritual with every new package of sandalwood incense, first coffee pour of the morning. Earliest spotting of a jogger in safety orange spandex. Vendors on the corner with rubber daisies, candy lips. First lap around the street fair ritual. Women in macramé tops, leather pants. Ritual of who to wave at, who to ignore.

This was before camera phones, so my roommate dragged along a digital and we had to pose and snap. I carried an oversized tumbler of lemonade, but my ice cubes did not quake. Bags upon bags of street crafts involving multicolor beads. Ritual of halving a Bavarian cream donut without a knife. Ritual of cursing my awful ex-boyfriend, spotted at the spun sugar stand in pink bro shorts. Banished like pumping out a flooded basement, dropping rental car keys into the afterhours slot. A Mylar balloon skewered by a branch when the ritual was complete.

Back at our apartment, my roommate's countdown to the school year was on its final fourteen calendar boxes. First day of semester outfits mapped on a dry erase board, discernible influence from *The Blair Witch Project*. Unseasonable heat ritual, undressing in front of the open fridge. Frozen top sheet. My roommate's chilled tank top. Ritual of the pre-semester instructor in-service pocket minibar. First swear word of the new academic year, casually deployed in a pedagogical lecture. My roommate renting a red convertible to cruise Lakeshore Drive in the final fringe of August light.

A Meaningful Contribution to the Profession

University Hall 309 is large enough for each graduate student to have a table and two chairs. Some tables are adjacent to electrical outlets, others include a view of the top half of a maple beginning its September shed. I'm in hot pink capris and one of my countless black nylon blouses, similar to what I might have worn to a nightclub in 1998 with white pleather booty shorts. At first I can't find my reading glasses and panic, but they are on my head. We all have a laugh.

This classroom is equipped with two industrial-sized rolls of paper towel, and a spray bottle of Virex sanitizer with a smiling opossum sticker over the lettering. It takes me a few minutes to connect to the Wi-Fi and load my slides. I close a browser where several tabs are open with searches for crust-free pie recipes and ergonomic patio furniture.

The academic job market is like a ravine with an indiscernible water source trickling at the bottom, I begin, then dim the lights.

Today's employment-seekers may find this hard to believe, but the MLA Job Information List (JIL) used to be an unwieldy and expensive print publication housed in a library. Sometimes the JIL was attached to a counter with a chain, like the hyperbolic chain wallet skaters once wore, occasionally so long they dragged on the ground and picked up stray pinecones. At times a JIL was shared between doctoral candidates for personal, off-campus use.

Perhaps we could imagine that two JIL-sharing doctoral candidates were engaged in the sort of relationship everyone lived to follow back before the internet was really a thing. This pair embodied a "beautiful ruins" trope commonly found in *fin de siècle* literature.

Did both smell like bonfire on Monday morning? Were they arguing about *Portrait of a Lady* in a study carrel? Did they bring one turkey croissant to campus in a single cooler bag and split it in the janitor's closet, adjourning to separate graduate assistant offices assigned loosely by cohort? Everyone knew which of them had purchased the JIL subscription, and it was not the more employable of the two.

[Skip over slide four, a thumbnail of my yesteryear self in a corduroy jacket, gazing hotly at someone just out of frame, pasted next to a bulleted list of cover letter best practices.]

You might think that naming a seasonal—and oftentimes vexing—employment clearinghouse after a woman would be a ticket to displeasing innuendo: *Hunkered down at the brew house with JIL and cried into my Bass ale all night*. Maybe someone would accuse her spouse of *thinking only of that bitch JIL*, while the burgeoning scholar made promises to JIL knowing intimately the limits of his intellectual prowess. Today, the JIL is simply called The MLA Job List. It's an online resource.

In a professionalization seminar of yesteryear, after a tutorial on requesting paper transcripts, my director of graduate studies Dr. XXXXX dedicated thirty minutes to the dilemma of back-to-back interviews with zero time to recharge via a protein snack. Take the stairs, peel the granola bar open like a banana and throat it, she advised.

[How thick were the granola bars back then? As thick as they needed to be, Candice.]

The JIL-sharing couple ended up in New York at the same time for MLA but never shared a small plate of gourmet cheeses or wandered the Strand or permitted themselves to grind against each other on the dance floor at The Limelight. Maybe he watched her wash her hair and then returned to his hotel room—shared with buddies from Lit Theory—and ate a CVS ham on rye.

Lore within their semi-selective R-1 institution suggested that the job seeker who purchased the JIL subscription ended up permanently ABD after an incident involving fire on the subway. Some speculate that the fire originated in a rucksack stuffed with a massive paper document.

[Minimize popup Teams notification: anonymous caller seeks urgent freelance French tutoring.]

At this point in my lecture, I pause and think about my graduate school roommate, and how we both landed a preliminary interview with St. XXXXX University at MLA San Diego. This was not one of those bull pen junkets where job-seekers loom in folding chairs, clutching stacks of vitae and cheat sheets, but a hotel interview where I felt more like an in-call entertainer than a wannabe assistant professor. As an added layer of complication, my roommate and I wore identical "power suits" as a gag that felt uproarious in Filene's Basement but plain weird in the 27th floor Hilton suite where I lurked waiting for my roommate's interview to end and mine to begin.

[Cue slide ten, accompanied by "Only Happy When it Rains" by Garbage. A few students begin bobbing their heads.]

Graduate College Exit Interview Response #3

What is one piece of constructive criticism that you would like to offer your graduate program?

Some of my classmates complained when the university announced that a major motion picture would be filmed on campus. They hijacked the seminar table and stuck slogans on posterboard smeared with rubber cement. I was only interested in the rubber cement, or rather the smell of it, which landed me back in Sister Mary Rita's third grade classroom full of tangled rosaries and hovering bees.

My students frothed with enthusiasm over the film, even if it was far more cerebral than anything they would ordinarily see, containing zero drag races or explosions. A talent scout roamed my Intro to Lit class, passing over Javier but signing Lisa with a promise that she would never have to work another shift at Donut Stop. My roommate disseminated a typed daily recap of which stars had been spotted on campus and where. I noticed that the elevators took twice as long and the restrooms were three times cleaner once filming began. We never spotted rats in the dining hall loading dock until the last of the movie trailers packed up.

I had trouble getting the students in Intro to Lit to focus. We were discussing "Car Crash While Hitchhiking" and Paul kept getting up to sharpen his pencil. But he was really gazing out the window at a man in black pinstripes who measured the distance between a trash can and a bench. My roommate was in our office typing up the latest: Dustin Hoffman spotted with an umbrella on Tuesday, unknown female star in gray trench coat observed holding a sandwich in University Hall lobby, rumors about a sequel or prequel or parallel universe thriller companion to the film.

The classmates with complaints staged a mild protest on the movie's release day, but nobody remembered their initial gripes, which were anti-capitalist but mainly anti-metafiction. I saw the film in the theater three times when it came out, looking for a glimpse of my legs on the quad or just thinking of how the air in the film was the same air I had breathed.

I had very few gripes of my own. Made peace with the Dean's spendy rooftop helipad, accepted the updated privacy policy, allowed myself to forget the temporary paper towel dispensers that vanished as soon as the film crew packed up. My face reddened inexplicably from the opening scene through the ending credits.

The Autumn Spark

Fall semester clocked in like a hung-over cashier. My roommate double-fisted dissertation hours, while I enrolled in a full load. Two classes overlapped by twenty minutes, which felt like a not-so-secret affair. Philosophy of Rhetoric, Wharton and James. Any time away from campus I spent attempting to read two books at once (one for each thigh).

I was dating a guy who thought bats hatched from seeds. Let's wash this beach blanket, he said, we might have picked something up from the trees. Beautiful like a roast beef sandwich. I had to stop my roommate from pinching him when he dozed on our secondhand divan, surrounded by my students' "Remembering Events" essays.

One autumn afternoon I was cramming two novels at once, boyfriend snoozing in the center of the living room floor. His garments swayed in a breeze from the ceiling fan, which only had one speed. I lingered simultaneously on a description of clams and a treatise on abjection. Then the party girls on floor twelve started tossing lit matches out their window.

We had to spend three hours on the curb. My roommate lugged a typewriter down the fire escape, bit the head off a gingerbread scarecrow. The boyfriend kept running hands through his hair, even though it had long ceased being cute. I imagined my student papers drifting into the flames, at this point merely a smolder, then hunkered one book into the crease of the other.

Battle Hymn of the Roommate

Sunday morning, and I was up early crying over a carpet shampoo named The Final Touch. Even the aggressive windowsill pigeons couldn't cheer me. People still had their flags out. I'd fallen asleep in full stage makeup. My roommate situated a heap of stargazer lilies in a vase and they were bleeding pollen onto untouched copies of *The New Yorker*. The issue on top boasted a dreamy purple cover but nobody wanted to read the story by Jonathan Franzen. We were collecting enough volumes to make a footstool.

I wanted to wash some grapes but had trouble turning on the lamp, which had been recently bedazzled and then stripped of bedazzling. My roommate was blasting The Prodigy and I muttered something about the security deposit, which might as well have been a sword, but then I needed my roommate to assist with removing the enormous set of adhesive eyelashes we'd experimented with the night before.

Students kept bragging about opulent foam parties downtown and I wanted in. Ever the buzzkill, my roommate insisted on being my "date." The foam-shooter erupted on a dais and my flimsy shift turned into the skin atop a forgotten pudding cup. Ian with the omnipresent pack of Big Red passed me a weird unlit pipe. The rest was fuzz, but somehow I made it into my duckling pajamas and removed my contact lenses. (Even wearing the skullcap of smack and bleeding from the mouth into a snowbank in high school I remembered to take out my contacts.)

So there I was, nauseous in the utility closet, cradling a bottle of The Final Touch like a dehydrated elderly cat. Many graduate students would need to explain such tears to a roommate: Dear Roommate, the name "the final touch" speaks to the liminality of existence, as one day we will deposit our last rent check in the red metal box, and hug each other before departing in separate directions, or maybe you'll be on a train and I'll be standing on the platform and realize *oh fuck, this is it*, and slap the glass but with gloves on so it makes no sound.

My roommate knew this without a word, however, and never purchased that brand of carpet shampoo again.

The Long Winter

Yes, sometimes we drifted into the fray of the parade and wound up kissing strangers and not in the way learned in French class, which wasn't "French kissing" but something akin to a vigorous handshake. Another stranger might offer beads or a bite of a cruller—warm from the bakery or from being transported via décolletage: nobody knew, and both were considered sanitary. When we visited the new dance club ("Imagination Cabaret"), a woman in the bathroom exclaimed my cuteness (just like Bjork!) then transferred the purple wig from her head to my head.

We purchased pre-owned negligées off the rack. Department store testers offered complimentary licks. My roommate started an apple cinnamon Nutri-Grain bar on the Brown Line then tired of it and passed me the stump. Philosophy professors employed the universal term "sloppy seconds" when explaining concepts to general education undergraduates. If you wanted to entice someone you'd fellate the drinking fountain stream and hope they were watching. Overnight taxi seats were wet when you sat on them and equally wet when you left.

So when we gather around the tablet this evening to scroll the latest, I can't help but think of all the roommates in their current confinement, half glad that they now constitute an official household, half wishing they had splurged on an extra set of emergency forks. I recall the winter that we nicknamed *The Long Winter*. Was it even that lengthy? My roommate helped me shimmy my feet into plastic bread bags before we shoved our rickety cart up Broadway to the Jewel-Osco in the snow. How would we entertain ourselves, we both wondered, and located the most complicated spritz cookie gun available to the general public of 1999.

I didn't begin crying until my roommate discovered the chickpeas sold out, all marshmallows flattened, and every copy of *People* damaged in transit. The buses still weren't running, but a guy we vaguely recognized let us squeeze into his car between salvaged recyclables and packed sharps containers. We vowed to start marking the days by the volume of our knitting.

Graduate College Exit Interview Response #11

Describe an instance where your coursework provided guidance for a non-academic situation.

At first we are both terrified of the seagull. I mistake it for someone's lost cropped t-shirt writhing in the wind. Students pass by on their way to a new bubble tea cart stationed outside University Hall. Every other customer demands an explanation of what bubble tea is before placing an order. My roommate and I step out of line and regard the seagull in its despair.

I never bonded with a bird until Fancy Pants, a pigeon that roosted against my office window when I had an awful library development job back in undergrad. Diminished by a pile of manila file folders, I settled my cheek against the window and hoped Fancy Pants would transmit compassion through the glass. That night at the bar, when my friends told stories about shoddily crafted sourdough loaves or making out with strangers on the bus, I told them about Fancy Pants and our bond.

Nowadays we could pull out anyone's cell phone and Google "seagull first aid," but in this moment outside University Hall nobody has the internet handy, so we improvise. Step one: assess the situation. We have a seagull in distress. There are problems with motion. There's a sound, like the time my neighborhood friends dragged a water-logged record player out of the retention pond and tried to play *Houses of the Holy* on it. I instinctively drop to the ground and approach the seagull, minimizing eye contact. My roommate trails behind, holding my purse.

I would have resigned from that library development job much earlier had it not been for Fancy Pants, who I referred to as "FP" after we got to know each other. Some days FP was there when I arrived at work, and others I had to wait until sun shifted to the other side of the building. My main tasks in library development were processing in-kind gifts and brewing herbal tea for my boss, who always found something to criticize in both areas. My handwriting was too slanted, my boiled water too frantic. I added FP to the library donor database and embossed several book plates with those initials. Looking back, I was probably dehydrated and depressed, maybe hallucinating. FP's feathers were exquisite, though—iridescent and layered like a psychedelic fondant dream.

If I feel a rapid kinship, it's hard to break. For instance, one time I rescued a toddler abandoned at a resort where I was cocktail waitressing. I jumped into the pool to fish the child out, soaking my polo dress and WonderBra, which never fully dried. As authorities carried the toddler away, we both sobbed as if she was my own child. Yet it takes several minutes of pressing the injured seagull to my chest before we connect. The poor bird is easy to catch, the beak is not difficult to avoid thanks to a spare bandanna, but my instincts stall as students gather and screeches become more urgent.

At that moment, my roommate recalls a kernel of wisdom from our linguistics seminar. It's something about every language fusing a stone with a saucer (roughly translated). I realize that I am examining the wrong side of the seagull. We ask for a few extra sets of hands, and cradle the bellowing fellow in a way that reveals his arctic bosom. It's there that I find a sparkly roach clip snagged on the underbelly. My roommate and I lock eyes, and I defer the act of unclipping.

When we release our mild ward at the memorial fountain on the east side of the University Hall plaza, he looks back at us with gratitude. My roommate produces a squirt bottle of vanilla hand sanitizer, which we rub up and down our arms. Then we line up for bubble tea and ask for the thickest possible gauge of tapioca.

Colorized Photo of My Roommate Doing What My Roommate Did Best

An impossible decision—which of the third-years would complete a flagship interview for *Today's Unionized Graduate Student Quarterly*. We all paid our dues. Some of us volunteered handing out trifold brochures. Others agitated the subway station along with Students for Zero Gravity and Animal Liberation Crüe. I copy edited seven hours of hysterical manifesto pro bono, curled ribbons for the card-signing lollipops. My roommate preferred direct debit and a showy, ambiguous floss jacket patch.

In our most heated forums, organizers debated the acceptable number of broken windows in a classroom, or the tendency of Student Health Services to malign us as overgrown undergraduates. Hanna was a shoo-in for the flagship interview. Cavalier, sharp-shouldered, emboldened by a multi-generational hedge fund she denounced after all her bills cleared. But somehow the union vice president settled on my roommate and would not acquiesce. The glamour, the height, fluency in both aesthetic theory and two-stroke engine repair, straight As on the transcript like a row of teeth that never needed cosmetic whitening.

Deliberations and refutations took place on an online bulletin board visited mostly by aspirational hackers. My roommate, as usual, was oblivious, victorious. I recall not the interview responses, which leaned on apocryphal Frank Zappa quotes and nautical metaphors, but my roommate's self-curated outfit for the photo shoot. Green felt bird-beak hat. Marabou cravat and matching novelty cufflinks. Checkerboard leggings and flowy striped boho oxford. Posed outside our apartment building with vendors and small children gawking. All reduced to gradients of black and white in the issue, which arrived in our graduate assistant mail slots six months later.

Approximately twenty-two years from that day, scrolling "Chicago's Most Painful Forgotten Moments" group on Facebook, putting off Adobe-signing graduate thesis defense forms queued in my workflow, two pit bulls snoring on either side of the kitchen table, and there it is, returned to resplendent candy counter surge of orange and green. A damp grenade in my ribcage. My roommate gazing off at something mid-sentence, mid-shutter. Ubiquitous platform boots, dangling Winston Ultra-Light. My fingertips buzzing like the idea of killer ants. Caption for the post: *Building circa 1918, residential, current status unknown.*

The One Where My Roommate Climbs Inside a Giant Crystal Ear and Falls Asleep

I take my roommate's face down to an alien green. "It's the universal neutral," my roommate says, "forget it's also the color of cash." The makeup sponges smell like cheap rubber gloves. I feel like a pharmacist and I'm into it, wearing an oxford shirt patterned with tiny Satan faces, white denim cutoffs from the husky boys section of Value Village. I build ravines into the sides of my roommate's face, apply adhesive freckles shaped like stars if viewed with a magnifying glass. When it's finally time to do my makeup we've both lost interest.

Most Chicagoans wouldn't be caught dead in a tourist trap like Navy Pier unless cheating on a spouse, hoping to roll undetected through novelty sucker shops and airbrush stands. The minute we step out of our cab we vow to speak only French. If we forget a phrase we laugh as we imagine tourists would. A balloon man tries out his best idioms on my roommate. A street hippie in tie-die knows we're faking and asks us each for a five. When we walk past the Shakespeare theater we mope, recalling literature field trips of yesteryear before we were ABD.

Around this point I meet a man selling petrified quail eggs. He's wearing a shirt we would now consider ripped straight from *The Sopranos*, but in that Navy Pier light he's an original hot beacon. My roommate busy applying a layer of Clinique Black Honey, I slip a few words in English to the man, as if breaking character mid-skit in honors French IV. My ghastly upper Midwestern accent like rubber cement that coats every petrified quail egg, drips down the man's goatee and glazes his circular shades.

Afterwards my roommate is nowhere to be found. Should I call out in English, or French? The petrified quail egg man writes a series of numbers on my hand in ball point, but they instantly sweat off in my frenzied search. I attempt to file a report with Navy Pier security, but the closest to a French speaker is Québécois Randy who has munched a hash blondie and stares at the lake with lust. He leaves me at the threshold of the "Human Body Illuminated" exhibit, and I call for my roommate, like a sea bird wailing for shore.

The One Where None of My Relevant Experience is Useful

It's funny what things from the past stick with us. To wit: I'm violently ill after delivering a keynote somewhere near Ocala, Florida. It's February 2020. I have eaten nothing unusual. Maybe I rolled my eyes extra hard when one of the hosts pitched her treatise on popular culture. But I only had one glass of wine after the lecture. Didn't sample crab dip prepared by the executive assistant who also arranged my lodging at a highway chain hotel with a pool in the courtyard.

I'm comfortable enough professionally that I only pack dull separates for this trip. Rather than eating in the panopticon hotel lobby, I stalk across a pedestrian-unfriendly berm to Wendy's. There might be some unsalted almonds in my pocket. But none of this poisons me, and nothing explains why at 5:06 pm I purchase a tie-dye beach dress from the hotel gift shop, dive into the pool, and float on my back in front of a family on vacation, the youngest in water wings, the mother gazing with horror at the way the beach dress barely covers my assets.

In a previous life I loved a piano bar. Didn't matter where it was, New York or Denver, when I walked through the door to behold the piano, goosebumps rode my arms like a sudden-onset rash. My graduate school roommate was a piano savant who could make even the drunkest Paula O'Malley sound like a seasoned crooner. It never took much to get me to sing. An amaretto sour barely had to touch my tongue, and I was slithering through "Mon mec à moi" with such authenticity that tourists tried out their French on me.

Of course, this highway motel near Ocala has no piano bar, but there's a man playing rhythm guitar poolside. According to a maintenance woman who later helps me reconstruct events, after the swim I wriggle out of the beach dress and trudge in my shapewear over to the sad excuse for a tiki cantina. A few minutes after my Diet Coke arrives, a minivan loses control on the nearby highway, breaches the guardrails, and bursts into flames mere yards from the hotel.

Nothing feels real as the smoke unfolds, the same way nothing felt real back in 1998, and maybe that's why I begin telling the rhythm guitar man (who I address as "Steely Dan") all about my PhD program back in Chicago so long ago. It's a good thing I'm still slightly hot because Steely Dan maintains interest and is a decent listener for someone who may be busking without a license and whose repertoire of songs is limited to "Sister Morphine" and "Ventura Highway." People from a nearby light industrial park gather on the hotel lawn to view the wreckage. It appears the minivan has no driver or passengers, which is impossible, but my mind is elsewhere.

I'm halfway through explaining the concept of pizza hours, or instructor in-service, where a graduate teaching assistant receives three credits toward maintaining full time status but does nothing to satisfy those credits, and this makes me realize I am starving and shaky, but I lean into it and start telling Steely Dan about a few notable takeaways from my lecture, then decide I need to run up to my room real quick so I can give him a signed copy of the event program.

When I return to my room—finally shoving the keycard in the right way after multiple attempts—light discharges through musty sheers. I steady myself on the shallow desk that might be more appropriate for awkward upright sex than for actual business activity. I realize I am about to get violently ill. I need to remember a phone number and I don't know why. The room has a landline phone but nowhere to plug it. I drag the shallow desk away from the wall and dig at the carpet.

I'm still in damp shapewear and the beach dress is missing, but at least I have my purse. This is one of my greatest virtues. Even the time I jumped off the merry go round, I made sure my crossbody was secured before letting go. Even when my roommate and I had to run from police that night at Dooley's, my leather lunch box purse never left my side.

I finally find the plug and plug in the phone. An instant dial tone. The zero button looks larger than all the others. It looks orange and the light wavers. I'm shuddering, hallucinating, unaware of the fact I'm hallucinating, and ask the hotel switchboard operator to put me through to "directory assistance," which he has no understanding of, and I halfheartedly start telling him about the concept of an operator, about the number you could call for the time, about dial-a-story from my hometown library, and then I start to sob because I miss my childhood dog, Chowder. The line clicks from silence to static.

I recall the time I vomited on Chowder's back in the middle of the night. She slunk away and hid behind my parents' amply stocked wine rack. Nobody noticed her there and kept wondering where the hidden barf smell was coming from. Dinner had been sausages and apples, my least favorite, as mixing of sweet and savory was something I rejected. It's amazing nobody strolled over to the wine rack seeking liquid encouragement, but maybe my parents already had several bottles or jugs open.

This memory makes me even more nauseous. I head to the bathroom and pass out, or some other lapse in time happens, because I wake with ceramic tile waffles on my cheek and can finally recall my old roommate's cell phone number. I cough myself across the floor and locate my phone, which is turned off for some reason, an unexpected blessing. I remember my locker combination from senior year of high school. I can picture Chowder in the box of puppies at the humane society and think of how I picked her because of the pink dash on her nose. The way she huddled against my neck. Her sweet smell, like a hayloft.

In the distance, a tow truck clears the remains of a burned-out Honda Odyssey.

Photos We Never Took in 1998

Searching for my birth certificate or a long-lost prescription for narcotic allergy tablets, I found my Swatch of yesteryear, cloaked in sticky resin and dissolved bands. My roommate always had to buckle it for me. Sometimes I carried an antique pocket watch that was semi-functional.

One night it snagged on the beer case at Buddy's Mart, after the candle festival, roping me between tropical wine coolers and Miller Lite. For a duo who dressed up two nights a week minimum, with an abundance of accessories, we took few photos aside from the cats: Pandora on the dining room table with a background of fog, Agnes entangled in a roll of polyester rickrack.

My roommate smoked indoors and crushed out every cigarette like a French nanny. More often than not, I was deep in a primitive version of fin-de-siècle cosplay. So today, reading *Station Eleven* in double masks at a taped-off table in a room that seats five hundred, a winter cloud tossing nonpareils onto the windowsill, I wonder if the beer case at Buddy's Mart was attempting some kind of warning.

To my roommate: avoid speedboats, speedballs, degree-granting programs in Denmark, fad diets involving canned pumpkin, greased hinges, yacht rock while intoxicated. To me: a year's worth of aggravating horoscopes, courtroom décor of the late 1970s, postcards arriving from unknown origin, heavy-breathing colleagues, math beyond comfort zone, dreams where my roommate was trapped on the other side of the glass.

The Girl with the Black Lipstick

Sometimes one strategic change is all it takes. For my roommate this was a leather briefcase. Not the kind my father filled with yellow legal pads and took to work selling machines. Nor the doctor's case I lugged on Halloween as a feminist statement orchestrated by my angry aunt. This case was so sexy you wanted to wear it. So raw you thought about eating it and felt both ashamed and ravenous. When my roommate carried that briefcase, everyone halted. Buses slowed at each intersection. The Chicago River burped like a Rush Street drunk. The briefcase was completely empty, but no one would ever know.

My favorite story has always been *The Little Match Girl*. In grad school I walked night streets and looked in windows at families and what was on their plates, which was often green and beige. While my roommate was shampooing the tassels of the leather briefcase, I walked up Sheridan in my black velour sweatsuit with the hood up, birding binoculars around my neck, ravaged by cold. My favorite family had two adults, three children, and an enormous white dog that looked like an exploding star. Above their door, a hand-whittled wooden dove.

There's a point in every degree program when some people become speakers and the rest either listeners or furniture. I overthought my style to the extent that I dreamt about crawling across a room-sized eyeshadow palette. My roommate took some photos we printed on proof pages, each one more mournful and gothic than the last. Ribbons singed with gas burner flame, Victorian novels buried in the park then exhumed after a fortnight. I wrote academic articles about wishing something existed in the heavens. My roommate was a speaker and I was a folding chair that nobody trusted to hold them up.

Every graduate student was required to attend two professional development events per semester. I preferred the series called "Rules of the Game," where Dr. March shared the latest academic dirt, digressing like an ant caught in a rivulet of Coke poured on a hot sidewalk. I was about to offer up tidbits gleaned when bartending a poststructuralist happy hour, but as soon as I opened my mouth the leather briefcase breached the seminar room doorway, followed by my roommate, blowsy and erudite. I swore I heard a faint ticking but it might have been my sinuses. "That's some bag," Dr. March said, "probably packed with knowledge."

Approximately seventeen years after that day and on the cusp of retirement, Dr. March would cold-call my administrative assistant, querying me to write an external promotion review. This was a decade after *Rules of the Game: The Monograph* was published by a minor Midwestern university press to slight acclaim. Following the established script, my admin told Dr. March I was encumbered with a series of essential meetings, then read out all the characters of a scheduling URL.

If only I could text my roommate about this missed connection, I thought, then put my creative dissertation (*The Girl with the Black Lipstick*) on indefinite hold through interlibrary loan.

Graduate College Exit Interview Response #5

How did university facilities and resources fortify your experience with graduate study?

You would think two people on the brink of holding terminal degrees could figure out how to install window coverings. We had to undo any customizations before moving out of our apartment, so the velvet draperies came down and cheap miniblinds needed to go up. But the instructions were the size of a fortune cookie fortune, blinds collapsing into themselves like dropped spaghetti. The drill's whinny reminded me of my favorite Laibach song, and I asked my roommate where that record was so I could cue it up.

Nothing was where it belonged. Leotards rammed into a sun tea pitcher, half my top-tier stuffed animals in hatboxes, the other half entombed in Tupperware. But my DJ bag was nowhere in the apartment, which meant only one thing. I had forgotten it in my university library study carrel and already turned in the key, per the pre-graduation separation checklist.

Giving up the carrel had been harder than kissing my TA desk goodbye or downing my last cup of putrid machine coffee. I had been on the study carrel waitlist for the entirety of my first two years in the program. While deferred, I seethed with jealousy as Erin McGeeney disappeared into her carrel with a stack of monographs and double pouch of red licorice. Trash-talked the losers who used their carrels solely for vodka storage or emergency hookups.

The day Locking Systems finally pressed the key to study carrel 3-003-9 into my palm I vowed to become the most grateful steward of resources. I would dust weekly, straighten daily. Did I sleep in there sometimes? Only on accident, face pressed into the ribcage of a boyfriend who had dozed off gorgeously on my interlibrary loan pile. My roommate had no desire for a carrel, finding various park benches suitable for any activity.

Along with the key card I had signed a triplicate form with policies regarding lost and unclaimed property, which would be stored in the university library bowels for a maximum of fifteen days. It had only been five days since I turned in the carrel key, but my roommate and I still exited the apartment evacuation-style upon the discovery of the missing bag. We hopped the first bus we saw, which happened to be the local that made stops at every tourist trap. My stomach shuddered as I thought of my records abandoned in some lost and found.

As a meditation, I pictured the liner notes of every record in the DJ bag. Recalled the order I left them in. Remembered why I had the bag on campus in the first place. (My students, raised on compact discs, wanted to touch real vinyl.) I shifted around in my bus seat and noticed something bulky in my roommate's tote. It wasn't a grinder sandwich or a hand mixer, but it was around that size. The bus slowed so tourists could descend on Water Tower Place. The beak of the drill emerged from beneath a sleeve of graham crackers. It reminded me of my stuffed animal kiwi bird, at that moment flattened in a hatbox between a bitchy novelty coffee mug and a pair of Carhartt socks.

We were too late to ask for assistance, the library help desk vacant. Nobody was around except a security guard huffing something out of a brown paper bag, and an undergraduate talking on the sole payphone on the first floor. My roommate slipped behind the counter, slid open a drawer, and produced a sub-master key. In the Employees

Only room, we stayed low and the drill withheld its loudest notes as cabinet brackets dropped one by one into my hand.

We caught the express home. I didn't even have to look inside the DJ bag to know everything was still there.

Acknowledgments

Grateful acknowledgment is made to the following journals where these stories previously appeared, sometimes in slightly different versions.

Always Crashing	Adventures of Mary Van Pelt A Very Decent Life Lady of the Canal The Problem of Summer
DIAGRAM	Battle Hymn of the Roommate Battle of Little Italy Gift of the Roommate Hot Tears The Long Winter
Does it Have Pockets?	Curator of the Year The Autumn Spark The One Where We Trick Tourists into Learning How to Dance Too Much Charge Trick Ethics

Flypaper	One for the Record Books
Gone Lawn	That Stuff is Going to Kill You
On the Seawall	More Harm than Good Late August Edition
Southern Indiana Review	Green and Infinite Story About the Sea Sweat Equity
West Trestle Review	Photos We Never Took in 1998

Much gratitude to my friends and colleagues for their support as I wrote this book: Christopher Barzak, Kate Christie, Mike Geither, David Giffels, Mary Grimm, Brittany LaPointe, Thea Ledendecker, Caryl Pagel, Hilary Plum, Theresa Procopio, Lisa Rhoades, Tricia Springstubb, David Todd, and Marie Vibbert. Special thanks to Amy Bracken Sparks and Susan Grimm, and to Sarah Freligh and Jenny Irish for their kind words about this book.

Eternal gratitude to Amy Freels and Diane Goettel, and to all the Black Lawrence Press family.

Abundant thanks and loud guitars to Julie Brooks Barbour. Love and gratitude to my parents, and to Eric, Gabi, and Ray.

And thanks to all the sweet, wild friends of yesteryear.

Permissions

Photo: Gabi Thompson

Mary Biddinger is the author of numerous books with Black Lawrence Press including *Partial Genius: Prose Poems* (2019), *Department of Elegy* (2022), and her debut work of fiction, *The Girl with the Black Lipstick* (2025). She has received awards and fellowships from the Cleveland Arts Prize, Ohio Arts Council, and National Endowment for the Arts. Biddinger teaches creative writing at the University of Akron and in the NEOMFA program, and serves as poetry editor for the University of Akron Press.